Erotic Bedtime Stories

Erotic Bedtime Stories

Erotic Bedtime Stories
Edited by: JA Lafrance
Formatted by: JA Lafrance
Published by: JA Lafrance
Cover by: JA Lafrance
Copyright © 2017 by JA Lafrance
Updated 2020

Erotic Bedtime Stories

Erotic Bedtime Stories

author of sassy strong women

JA
Lafrance

Blurb

Do you need to be seduced into a peaceful sleep, with naughty dreams and peaceful nights?

Erotic Bedtime Stories will lead you into a path of temptation, as it helps flourish your fantasies and inspire your realities.

Dive into the erotic stories and let your dreams become X-rated, as you seek out your pleasure before falling asleep.

Warning: For mature audiences only. Contains language and actions some may deem offensive. Sexually explicit content. Ménage, BDSM, MF

Erotic Bedtime Stories

Books By JA Lafrance

Curvy and Wanted
The ECE & Her Billionaire
The Brother & Her Best Friend
The Girl & Her Men
The Daughter & Her Athlete (Coming
Soon)
Bleeding Miners MC
From the Darkness
Comes the Light (Coming Soon)
Others
Erotic Bedtime Story
Poetry of Emotions, Trust, Respect, and
Yearning
Stunned
Her Stern Rancher
Yes I'm Ready
For What It's Worth
Unhinged Thoughts: An Erotic Thriller
A Curvy Kind of Love

Erotic Bedtime Stories

Contents

Acknowledgments

FIRST, I'D LIKE TO thank every one of you for picking up my book. I'd like to make this acknowledgment not about the people who helped to make my imagination fly but to everyone. It doesn't matter what your sexual preference is, all that matters is that you are truly in the moment and enjoy every aspect of your experience.

Whether you are, a Dominant and have a beautiful submissive, or a person who enjoys being tied up, maybe just a person who loves the intimate feeling of being close to your partner.

Whatever category you fall into embrace the connection and enjoy your experience, because in the end we are all different and different is good.

Claiming My Pet

"The fact that I can see you in my head, and the first place I see you is in my room spread out on my bed, it's so cute and extremely hot." He whispers.

"Then you get that look in your eyes, and it's the best feeling ever. It tells me you want me." His voice is getting louder.

"My Pet, I need you to keep that look in your eyes when I tell you what I am going to do to you tonight." My Master says as he caresses my cheek and stares into my eyes.

I nod my head. The anticipation is radiating through my body. My heart is pounding. My breathing has increased and I am trembling.

"First my Pet, I am going to bind your arms, from your wrists to your

9

elbows." He says with a shine in his eyes and his voice lowers.

"Then I am going to bind your legs from your knees to your ankles." His voice has now turned husky, and he has not taken his eyes off of mine.

"I will make you kneel on the bed and bind your arms to your body and place you on my bed, with your ass in the air." He whispers and his breathing has increased slowly, but steadily.

My eyes shine with lust that I have for my Master. As his, shine brightly with lust and something that I have never seen on a man.

"Then I am going to mark what is mine with my hand. Redden your ass with my hand print." His husky voice is making my body burn with need.

He pulls rope from behind his back. He gently runs the rope down my arms and slides one of my hands through a loop he has made. The loop is big enough for both my hands to slide in.

"Bring your hands together my Pet."
He whispers. He proceeds to tie the rope
around my wrists snuggly. It's the perfect
fit not to tight but also not loose enough to
get free. He twines the ropes around my
arms making crisscrosses up to my elbows
and tightens the rope, placing my hands
in a prayer position.

"Stand up, my Pet!" he demands. I
stand with my legs shoulder width apart,
and my eyes locked on my Master.

"My Pet, walk closer to the bed and
stand with your legs together." He states
in a husky voice.

I walk towards the bed, turn and
face him. Making sure my eyes connect
with his.

He groans and adjusts himself,
while slowly prowling towards me.

"You are always so eager to please
me, my Pet." He hums in my ear.

I give him a small smile and watch
as he lowers himself to the floor. He
inhales and growls. Tying my ankles with
the same loop that he did with my wrists

and then demanding that I "place my other foot in the loop". I do as he asks, and he tightens the rope and then makes the same crisscross pattern up to my knees. The silk of the rope has my body humming with need. What's turning me on even more is that my Master is on his knees in front of me. His face is close to the lips of my pussy, and he is taking deep breaths, nothing else just steady deep breathing and groaning his appreciation.

He slowly stands allowing his hands to lightly drag up the inside of my thighs. With feather-light touches he runs his finger over my sensitive bundle of nerves, but doesn't add enough pressure to feel anything other than a light touch.

"Pet, on your knees please." He whispers seductively into my ear and then runs his tongue from my ear down to my pulse point and bites my neck with a growl. I shudder and slowly lower to the floor. Master has his hand on my arm, so I don't fall and once I am effectively on the floor he moves in front of me.

Erotic Bedtime Stories

"Eyes on me Pet" he states. I look up into his eyes and notice his arms move slowly down his body to his belt buckle, and then he whispers, I want your lips wrapped around my cock, Pet. I want to see those glossy lips sliding up and down my shaft as I pump into your mouth. Your saliva on my cock will please me in abundance. Will you do that for me? Let me feel your mouth on my cock?" He asks me. I nod in agreement and lick my lips. I have wanted to taste his cock since we walked into this room.

He undoes his pants and pushes them down past his knees. He is just about to step out of his pants when I lose my restraint and lunge forward attaching my mouth around the head of his cock. He groans and then pulls out and looks at me sternly "That Pet has earned you two swats of my hand on the pretty ass of yours. You will wait until I give you permission to take my cock." Then he steps out of his pants and neatly places them on the chair behind him.

"Now Pet, firstly you are going to run your tongue up the length of my cock, and then you will take the head into your mouth and taste me. Now stick out your tongue." Master states and moves close to me; his cock is placed in front of my mouth and I stick my tongue out and starting at the base of his cock. I slide up the length with my full tongue pressed to his shaft and then take the tip of his cock into my mouth. I add a little suck before slowly descending the length of his shaft as far as I can go without taking him into my throat.

Master is groaning when I come up and whispers "Take me as deep as you can go. Swallow my cock Pet." And then lets his head drop backwards and groans. I take my time lowering down his shaft again. This time when his head hits my throat I swallow and allow him to go deeper. He groans as I slide up and suck making him growl. I start to bob my head up and down his shaft. His reaction to my movements is to make his body stiffen. I

14

can feel his cock lengthen and I know he
is on the verge of coming down my throat
when he hollers "STOP!" and pulls his
cock free of my mouth.

"I'd love nothing more than to come
down your throat Pet, but I will be inside
your tight body when you get my come."
His voice is stern but his eyes show lust
and power.

He guides my body up into a
standing position and turns me to face the
bed. "Pet, I am taking my pleasure from
this. You will come once I have taken my
pleasure and you will only do it then. If
you come beforehand, I will pull out and
you will finish me with your mouth."
Master sternly says. He takes another
length of rope and ties my arms tight to
my body. He places a tiny kiss on each
shoulder and runs his tongue along the
tops of each breast.

"Now Pet, kneel on the bed and
place your head on the mattress. I want
you to present me that pretty ass of
yours." He pushes me down on the bed

and brings my legs and hips so that they are flush with the edge of the bed.

My body is thrumming with desire for Master, I'm wet and my nipples are sensitive peaks. Master has taken control from here on out and his demanding tone has me waiting impatiently to see what his next move will be. I am blind to his movements now, but I can hear him quickly moving around the room.

Music starts to play in the room; it's a song that I haven't heard before. "Master, what is this song and who is it sung by?" I whisper into the open room. I can hear him approach the bed, and he whispers in my arched back "Pet it's called "Yes Boss" by Hess is More. They are not very well known but this song is one I happen to love." Then he gets up and leaves the bed.

"Pet, I have an anal plug here that I am going to insert into you. Then I am going to give you five spanks on your perfect ass. After I mark you as mine I am going to fuck you so hard. You will not

Erotic Bedtime Stories

come until I have taken my pleasure, do you understand?" He says and I feel cold gel squirt onto my ass, which causes me to jerk forward.

"Easy Pet, I'll warm you up" he states as he runs his finger down my crack and gently massages his finger around my anus. It causes me to moan and push back into his hand.

He drags his finger away and places a cold metal object at my opening. "Now Pet I am going to slowly work in this plug, it will burn at first but you need to relax and not strain. Once it is in you will feel pleasure, but will not take it." Master states as he slowly pushes into me. I moan, as I feel the burn from him pushing past my tight ring with the plug. The pleasure is taking the pain away. I want him to go quicker; I need him to move faster, so I beg, "Please Master, faster" and then let out a loud moan.

"You will not cum my Pet, that will happen at my hand and only after I have finished inside you". Masters stern tone turns me on even more. Just as I am getting used to the plug in my ass, I feel a sharp smack on my ass cheek and hear Master demand "COUNT PET!"

"One Master" I moan out and my body tightens. Then two quick smacks land on opposite cheeks and I scream and then state "Two, Three Master".

I am breathing heavy. I don't know who said that spankings are a punishment. His hand on my ass is turning me on. The burn from the smack has my body trembling with anticipation. I am brought out of my thoughts when another smack lands on my cheek and I moan and say, "Four Master" and start to squirm.

"Pet you WILL NOT come, do you understand me?" He questions and I nod my head. "You need to use your words, NOW answer my question.

"Yes Master, I will not come. You can have your pleasure." I say with a husky voice.

SMACK. "Five Master" and before I have even finished my count he has slammed his length deep inside me and groans. "Pet you are so tight and wet." And then starts to hammer in and out of me. His firm grip on my hips is going to leave bruises on them. His hard cock which is pounding into me will leave me walking funny for weeks and his groaning will leave the sound in my head for months. It is so erotic, that I can feel my body tighten more. My pussy is slowly pulsing, and all of a sudden, he stops and demands "You will not come Pet, my pleasure not yours" and then slams in hard.

Master starts to get harder again. I can feel his already hard cock get harder and lengthen inside me. His strokes start to go erratic, and then he stills and yells my name as his come coats the inside of me.

As soon as he starts to come back to earth his hand reaches around, and he presses hard on my clit and starts circling. "Come now Pet!" he demands and that is all I need I splinter into ecstasy, bright lights flash before my eyes and I can hear my voice echo of the walls in the room. "YES! Pet squeeze my cock!" Master demands and I come again squirting my juices all over Master and his cock.

I feel the ropes being loosened from my legs and Master whispers to me to sit up. He grabs my arms and guides me to a sitting position and holds me still while he undoes the rope.

As soon as the ropes are free he picks me up and carries me to the head of the bed. He lies me down on my side on the pillow and disappears to the en suite. I hear the water run and then Master is back placing a warm cloth between my legs and cleaning up his orgasm. I feel the bed dip and the covers are taken from underneath me. Then they are over me, and he whispers into my ear "Sleep Pet, remember I will always be watching you" and he places a kiss on cheek. That is all I remember before passing out cold.

Erotic Bedtime Stories

I awake in the morning expecting to
still be wrapped up in my Master's arms,
but he is gone. I get out of bed and wrap
the sheet around my body and walk out to
the living room.

In the living room, there is a table
set with pancakes, sausage, scrambled
eggs, coffee, and orange juice. But still not
note. I sit down and start to eat when
there is a knock on the door.

When I look through the peephole
nobody is there. I open the door and on
the floor, is a box. I bend down and scoop
the box up and bring it inside the room. I
sit on the couch and look at the box. On
top of the box is a stock card that says,
"Wear me always", so I lift the lid of the
box and find a diamond encrusted collar
with "PET" spelled out in sapphires front
and center. I lift it out of the box and place
it around my neck. My Master has just
claimed me as his Pet.

Mysterious Room

In the middle of the night, in a room I am unfamiliar with sits a man in a suit. His body is facing the bed but it is shadowed by darkness.

From my position on the bed I can't see his face. I know I am cuffed to the headboard and I have a ball gag in my mouth.

My heart is pounding, my breathing is erratic and my body is trembling.

I wonder if I am trembling out of fear or if I am cold. The air in the room is chilled. I look down my body and notice I am in my black lace bra that holds my DD's and my matching lace thong. My feet are still in my satin black stilettos.

I hear movement around where the man is sitting as he stands from the chair. It's still too dark to see his face, but he

22

whispers, "You've been bad, a very bad girl Sweets". That voice, it's so smooth with the hint of an accent that I can't place. His movements suggest that he is taking off his belt.

He steps closer to the bed I am on and demands "Flip on your side". I pause and think how am I going to do this? "NOW" he demands in a stronger voice. So, I roll on my side away from him. My arms are twisted above my head. My head and my shoulders are feeling the strain.

"Sweets, you weren't supposed to be in that club. For your indiscretions, you shall get ten lashes of my belt. You must count and you must count loud. Understand?" he whispers in my ear as he reaches to take the ball out of my mouth. I nod my head, but he says, "No Sweets, I need your words."

"Yes" I whisper.

"Sweets, louder and you must remember who I am." He growls.

"Yes Sir." I say with a bit more force.

"You will do good to remember that Sweets," As he connects, with the first lash of the belt on my left ass cheek.

I scream out as if I am in pain. It's a touch pain with a bit of burn, but the groan from Sir is enough to keep me going.

"COUNT SWEETS!" Sir demands.

"One" I say, and he tells me "You forgot something, Sweets." So I whimper out "One Sir, Sorry Sir".

Just as I am relaxing back into the bed I get hit harder with two quick cracks of the belt. "Two Sir, Three Sir" I moan.

"Sweets you are looking beautiful with my marks on you" he says in a low husky voice.

Then I get hit again with another two quick lashes of the belt. The pain is gone now. I am moaning and trying to rub my thighs together to relieve some of the ache.

"Don't move those thighs Sweets, your pleasure belongs to me. I will decide when you come. Right now, you will come much later. NOW COUNT!" he sternly states.

"Four Sir, Five Sir" I say and fight the moan that is threatening to slip from between my lips.

Crack, Crack, Crack. "Five Sir, Six Sir, and Seven Sir" this time I can't hold the moan that comes out.

"Sweets, are you wet for your Sir? Do you feel that building need in the pit of your stomach, the need to come to release? That feeling is mine and you will do good to listen to me and hold on tight" he whispers in my ear as he rubs his hand around the heat that the belt as left.

He moans and whispers to himself "Seeing these welts, the red marks and hearing the moans coming from your mouth has made me hard Sweets."

I whimper I don't know if I will be able to hold on. My orgasm is building and a few more hits from his belt will push me over the edge.

CRACK. "Eight Sir", I say and then tell him "Sir, I need to come, please let me come!"

"If you cum Sweets, before I get my cock deep inside you, I will add five more lashes of my belt to your punishment, do you understand?" He says and then Crack. "Nine Sir".

I have to fight the building need. Then Sir leans down and runs his tongue along the welt and places a kiss on my red mark. "Sweets, you taste so sweet." He whispers.

Crack! "Ten Sir" I yell, I need to come, Sir needs to hurry.

He walks around to the side I am facing. His face is still hidden by the dark, but his rock-hard erection is straining in his dress pants.

"Sweets, how do you feel?" he asks. I am just about to tell him to hurry up and fuck me when I notice that his hands are on the buttons of his pants. He is undoing his pants. As he slides his zipper down, I notice the head of his cock is sitting at the top waiting to fall from the confines of his pants.

He pulls his pants down. As his pants come down his cock stays fully erect pointing up as if he is saluting me and demands "Open your mouth Sweets!"

I open my mouth and lick my lips as he kneels on the bed. His face is still in the dark but his cock is at my lips as he pushes into my mouth. He pushes until he feels me gag, and then he slides back out. He repeats this process until I start to feel him lengthen. I take it upon myself to take Sir deeper into my throat and suck as hard as I can and then I pull back, because he has withdrawn from my mouth.

"Sweets that was naughty, I think it's my turn" he says with an evil chuckle in his voice then pushes my legs over, so I am lying on my back. I think he is going to leave me like that and just climb on, but her reaches for an ankle strap and placed my left ankle in it. He repeats the same process on the right foot.

I am laying spread on the bed for Sir; he is slowly and seductively removing his clothing. I still can't see his face, but his body is amazing. He has a six-pack and his skin is sun kissed. He runs his hands down his body and I follow with my eyes. I notice the "V" that points to the erect cock. I can't wait for it to be inside me.

"Please Sir, I need you" I beg. Which causes him to chuckle and say "Soon Sweets, you teased me with your mouth now it's my turn to tease you."

He reaches into the bed side table and comes out with a blindfold. He places the blindfold over my eyes and whispers in my ear "Just feel Sweets."

I hear him walk towards my feet, the bed dips in between my spread legs and I feel his wet tongue sliding up the inside of my right leg until he hits my knee. He switches over to the left leg and continues from my knee to my thigh. He gently places a kiss on my pelvis and then runs

his tongue down my slit, dipping in to find
my clit and down to my hole.

He is on his way back up to my clit
when I hear a buzzing and feel a vibrator
being pushed inside me. He then says,
"Don't cum Sweets, just feel" and sucks
my clit into his mouth.

I moan loudly and fight with my
body to listen to what Sir says. "Please Sir,
please let me come", I plead. I am in pure
torture hell right now. I need to release
but I have the overwhelming need to listen
to Sir.

I feel the vibrator being pulled from
my pussy and his mouth is moving away. I
moan from the absence of the constant
torture, but Sir's cock is there. He bends
over me and whispers, "Sweets, when I
enter you I want you to come. Then I will
fuck you harder and harder until I get two
more orgasms out of you."

Then he pushes inside me as deep
as he can go and I release. I moan and
come so hard that I am seeing white
lights. He doesn't stop to feel. He starts off

with a hard pounding pace that rolls a second orgasm into a third. I am trying to catch my breath. My legs feel like they are just lying limp on the bed. My arms are trembling and my breathing is fast.

His pace is still like a jackhammer, and he is bringing on another orgasm. Then all of a sudden, he pulls out of me. He rips the restraints off and flips me over onto my stomach and demands "Get up on your knees now!"

I follow instructions and am up on my knees when he says, "Have you ever had a cock in your ass?"

"No Sir", I tell him, and then he groans and says, "I will train you for that and soon I am going to fuck your ass"

Then he pounds back into me at a hard pace. My orgasm blindsides me and as it hits me, I hear him groan and I feel him lengthen inside me as his orgasm crashes through.

He collapses on top of me and rolls so that I am facing away from him, and he cuddles into me. He whispers, "Go to sleep

Sweets" and that is all I need. I am out like a light.

I wake in the morning to a cold bed beside me. A warm coffee and a muffin on the bedside table and a note that reads:

"Until we meet again sweets, Stay safe. I'll be watching you."

Two Masters

I don I always get roped into coming to this club. I figured after my last time my friend would understand my need to stay away.

Here I am sitting on a couch; to my left is my friend and her Master. He is sitting on the couch with his dress pants pulled down around his thighs, and she is on her knees, in between his legs with her bright pink lips wrapped around his cock.

31

To my right is a buxom blonde with her dress hiked up around her waist and her clean-shaven pussy on full display while her man is on his knees between her widespread legs.

"Honey, you need to show your Mistress how much you appreciate her body, you need to eat my pussy." The blonde demands her man.

I look away letting my eyes roam around the room. So many people are in various states of dress and various positions of sex.

My view is blocked by a pair of muscular legs in dress pants. I look up and into a set of green eyes with flecks of yellow and brown in them. They are locked on my hazel eye and my lips slightly part. His lips quirk up to one side in a half smile.

I hear a throat clear from behind the man, and standing there is another man roughly the same size and build as the first man, but his eyes are a clear blue and his face is what I would classify as boy next door.

"Well Gorgeous, looks like you have been chosen. Stand and let me get a look at my flavor for tonight." Blue eyes demand.

I jump in my seat, not sure I heard him correctly. It's hard to hear with the moans that are going on beside me.

"That's one Gorgeous," Blue eyes states sternly.

Green eyes quirk his eyebrow and gives a chuckle from his luscious mouth.

I uncross my legs, forgetting how short my dress is and flash the entire room my G-string as I stand. My face flames when I hear two growls coming from the men standing in front of me.

"That's three, one for that short of a dress, and one for flashing the room what I will be inside tonight" Blue eyes growls out.

The man with the green eyes has not said a word to me. He just stares at me, until I stand, and then he moves to my side.

"We are going to sit at the bar and talk to our partners." He says as he places his hand on my elbow and guides me towards two stools.

Both men sit on the stools then Blue eyes demands "On your knees, and keep your eyes down." I stand there a bit confused at what he just said. I look between the two men when green eyes growls and Blue eyes states "That's 4" and chuckles as I drop to my knees. I notice both men are straining their dress pants around the crotch region, but so is every other man around.

Blue eyes starts talking to a man to his left as green eyes is staring directly at me, I can feel his eyes on my bowed head.

Another man comes up behind me and stands extremely close to my head. He starts to play with my hair; he is running his hands through it and bringing strands of it to fall across the bulge in his pants.

Erotic Bedtime Stories

Green eyes growl low in his throat which snaps Blue eyes attention back to me.

"What. The. Ever. Loving. Fuck do you think you are doing Watson. What gave you the thought that you can touch what is ours?" Blue eyes yells at the man.

Green eyes reaches down grabbing a hold of my arm, hauling me up from my knees. He is dragging me to the hall down from where the bar was. It looks like two rooms back here. "Where are you taking me?" I whisper to Green eyes, to which he growls at me.

He slams open a door, and we are in a room, there is no bed but there is this huge wooden X thing against the wall, beside it is a rack full of what look like medieval torture device.

The door slams behind me causing my body to snap to attention. I turn to see Blue eyes glaring at me.

"Take your clothing off NOW!" he demands. I stumble, I really don't like to be demanded to do things.

"NOW! Gorgeous, you have five whips of my flogger heading your way. I can't wait to see you strung up on that cross with our marks on the inside of your creamy white thighs." Blue eyes states.

I start to undress when I notice Blue eyes whispering into green eyes ear and all he does is nod. Why doesn't he talk, is he mute? I think to myself. I am completely naked standing in the middle of this room.

As green eyes stalks over to me and places his hand on my elbow and guides me to the wooden cross. I look at it and wonder what the heck it is. In each corner, there are leather cuffs with buckles attached to chains that are bolted to the wood.

Green eyes spin me around and placed my back against the cold wood. I tremble at the sudden chill and feel his hand gliding down to my wrist as he grabs it and guides the wrist towards the leather cuff in the left, and then he does the same with the right. He steps away and adjusts himself.

Erotic Bedtime Stories

I watch as blue eyes steps up,
placing feather-light touches on my hip
and gliding his fingers down to my legs
grabbing a hold of my ankles. He places
both ankles in the cuffs and starts placing
tiny kisses up my legs. He reaches the
apex of my thighs and inhales, then
moans.

"Gorgeous, you smell appetizing" he
groans and then steps away.

I am trembling in anticipation,
waiting for their next moves. My heart is
pounding in my chest and my breaths are
coming in short pants through my open
lips.

"Now you have a punishment to
serve five whips from my favorite flogger.
You will count and address us
appropriately. Understood?" Blue eyes
states.

I nod my head to which he
responds, "I need words Gorgeous."

"Yes Master" I whisper.

"Louder Gorgeous," Blue eyes
demands.

"Yes Master" I state firmly.

He walks over to the shelf that holds the punishment sticks, but when he opens it I see ropes, canes and something that has a handle looks like ropes with knots attached to it and then I see him reach for another handle with what looks like strips of leather attached and brings it towards me.

"This Gorgeous is my favorite flogger" he says as he runs it gently up the inside of my leg.

Then suddenly as he gets to my left thigh he pulls back and strikes me hard. I scream at the sudden sting against my leg and state "One Master".

Blue eyes turn to Green eyes and hands him the flogger. Green eyes smiles as he takes the device and walks over to me running the flogger up my other leg, again when he gets to my thigh he pulls back at strikes it, with another sting, a groan slips from my mouth and I state "Two Master".

Green eyes smile at me then steps
back and hands the flogger back.

I anticipate the next strike from
Blue eyes and moan when he lands his
strike, and I yell "Three Master".

I watch as blue eyes hands the
flogger to green eyes; he takes it and lands
two quick and hard lashes against my
thighs, with a moan I tell him "Four
Master, Five Master".

Green eyes steps away to a chair in
the corner and sits down while he starts to
undress.

Blue eyes, who has already gotten
naked, drops to his knees in front of me
and latches his mouth onto my clit
sucking the bundle of nerves into his
mouth. I moan "Yes Master" and he looks
up at me and smiles, then whispers "Come
for me Gorgeous". That's all the
instruction I need and as he slides his
tongue back down my orgasm hits me
with such force that I squirt my juices all
over his face. I am shaking and breathing
heavily. When I am undone from the cross

39

and placed on a bed, which suddenly appeared, I am still excited but tired at the same time.

As green eyes lays on his back beside me, reaching over and grab my waist rolling me over so I am on top of him. His rock-hard cock is covered in a condom and instead of easing me onto his erection he pounds me down on him, and we both groan. He sets a hard pounding pace slamming into me over and over again.

Just as blue eyes comes over, stands with his erection at my mouth and demands, "Suck it Gorgeous".

I wrap my lips around the tip of his cock, just as green eyes slams into me forcing me to take the whole length of Blue eyes' cock into my mouth, deep and I gag.

Both my Masters moan in unison.

Green eyes have started a jackhammer pace while Blue eyes has stepped back to watch the show.

I cum so hard again as Green eyes increases his pace to hard and fast. It's such an intense orgasm that I stop breathing for a quick second to be brought back when Green eyes groans loudly slams into me and comes with such force I can feel the jets of come hitting my insides with the condom catching it.

Before I can catch my breath, I am lifted off Green eyes and placed against the nearest wall. Blue eyes guide his condom covered erection into me, and starts a steady pace. His strokes are bringing on another Orgasm and instead of slowing down he speeds up through my orgasm which causes another orgasm to crash through my body, milking his cock of every ounce of come he has.

I am spent; I lay my head on his shoulder and close my eyes. I feel him lay me down on the bed next to green eyes.

Green eyes roll into me and just as sleep takes over I hear Green eyes whisper "Sleep Sweets" and I am sound asleep.

I wake up in the morning to a coffee and a muffin on the bedside table.

In the Hotel

I am just arriving at the hotel when this stunningly gorgeous man with deep blue eyes walks up to me and whispers in my ear, "You will be mine tonight" and walks away.

He did not introduce himself just stated his intentions and walked away. I don't know what kind of woman he thought I was, but his intentions will not be fulfilled.

So, I yell at him "Keep dreaming honey!" and make my way to the front desk to check in.

I don't notice the man turn around with an angry expression or the fact that he turns to the concierge and points at me.

I have been in my room for all of ten minutes when there is a knock on the door. I look through the peephole and see the concierge that greeted me at the door.

When I open the door, he hands me a box and a note then turns and stalks away.

I closed the door and sit the box on the bed and open the note, which reads "You earned five lashes of my belt for that statement. Wear the items in the box tonight and meet me down in the lobby at seven pm sharp." I chuckle to myself and look in the box. The box has a black lace corset, a garter belt with black nylons and a pair of clear stilettos that have to be four inches high. I like the look of everything so this is perfect.

At six forty-five pm I am making my way down to get something to eat; I am wearing the stuff from the box under a black wrap dress. I don't expect to see my mysterious man but I don't have any hope he will go for me once he actually sees that my body isn't perfect.

I have just stepped off the elevator when my eyes come in contact with the same blue eyes as when I checked in, only he is standing with a beautiful blonde who is rubbing her hands up and down his arms. I throw a smirk at him and wave as I walk towards the bar.

I have just sat down at the bar and ordered my glass of red wine when the bartender walks over and takes my wine from me before I can take a sip; he also places a note in front of me. I yell "What. The. Hell?" and pick up the note.

"You have earned two more lashes with that display. Stand up now and walk towards the exit. I am waiting." I shake my head and look at the bartender, "Can I have my wine now please?" I ask. He says, "NO GO!" I give him the dirtiest look and get up and leave. There are other places around here.

Just as I exit the bar I feel a hand on my waist, and I am pulled into a muscular body. "You will listen to my every word Kitten" he states and starts to walk forward with his arm still around my waist.

Erotic Bedtime Stories

His grip is tight but soothing; his
steady breathing in my ear and his scent
is intoxicating it has me totally turned on.
        We are standing there waiting for
the elevator to arrive when I ask "What is
your name?" and he answers "To you it's
Sir, that's all you need to know for now"
and then he walks us forward onto the
cart.
        As the doors close he let's go of my
waist and demands "On your knees now
and keep your eyes on the floor" my eyes
flash to his, and he stares deeply into my
eyes before saying "NOW Kitten". I drop
my eyes to the floor and drop to my knees;
I don't know what emotion to let through. I
am extremely turned on but also a little
embarrassed that this unknown man can
state a command and I snap to his
attention.
        The elevator reaches the top floor
and Sir says in a firm voice, "Keep your
eyes down but stand". I do as I am told,
standing when I feel a cold piece of leather
being slipped around my neck. From my

downcast view, I can see this leather is attached to a chain that Sir is holding. He leads me out of the elevator by the chain, and we walk into a suite.

He tells me "Go through the door on your left and take that dress off. Get on your knees with your eyes down and wait for your punishment. Punishment before Pleasure Kitten and I intend to make you purr for me" and then he slaps my ass as I walk by him towards the door.

I have been kneeling on the floor for what seems like hours. Sir saunters into the room and groans. I don't know what he is doing but I can hear a bag unzip, and then he crouches down in front of me and whispers in my ear, "I am going to blindfold you now kitten", and then places a black blindfold over my eyes and I hear him take a step back. He then demands for me and takes my elbow to help me stand and then runs his hand down my arm to interlock our fingers, and we start to walk. He stops me and then I hear the springs on the bed creak and I assume that he has sat down. I feel him tug on my arm and guides me down just as his husky voice says "I am placing you across my knee Kitten; I've decided to use my hand instead of my belt for your punishment. My hand print on your ass will be the most beautiful site I've seen in a long time."

"Now Kitten, every time I spank you, I need you to count nice and loud for me. Make sure you address me as Sir, every time" he says and follows through with a loud smack on my ass, I yelp a little but don't say anything. "Did you forget already Kitten?" he growls. I shake my head and say really low "One Sir". I am tense from the first slap and Sir can feel it. "Relax Kitten I promise you, your pleasure will be given by me just as soon as we are done" he whispers and then his hand comes down again two times in a row alternating between cheeks. The second slap has me moaning, because now the burn has turned into a spike of pleasure. "Two, Three Sir" I say.

Now I can feel myself getting extremely wet. This man has my head and body in a trans, from the way he smells to his strong hands, he is turning me on and I have never experienced it this way before. I am brought out of my thoughts by three consecutive slaps on my cheeks. "Four, Five, Six Sir" I moan.

"I want you to stand up after my next slap. I am going to remove my pants and then I am going to get you to sit on my cock and let my fingers bring you to orgasm. I want to feel you come around me" he tells me and then his hand comes down hard, and I am placed on my feet while I hear him rustling to remove his pants, I hear the bed springs creak against his weight and then I am brought down hard onto his length, which brings my orgasm crashing through me and I scream out "YES SIR!" To wish I hear the sexiest groan and a "fuck yeah".

Once I come back to earth I am placed on my feet and turned to face the bed. The blindfold is taken off, and he whispers in my ear, "Get on all fours and present your ass to me Kitten."

I do as he says and kneel on the bed; I arch my back to show him my ass, and he groans and then whispers, "My Kitten and her perfect ass" and then slams his cock into me.

"My Kitten, I have a vibrating anal plug that I am going to insert in your" he says and then I hear the flip of a cap and cold gel hits my anus. He uses the anal plug to rub the gel around and starts to slowly push into my tight hole. He turns the vibrator on and then his hands are back on my hips, he starts a hard and fast pounding pace.

It is a matter of seconds, when he brings me to my second and third orgasm. It leaves me gasping for air and shaking from the sheer power of his thrusts.

I am on the verge of yet another orgasm when he slams into me hard and his middle finger lands on my clit, I can feel his powerful orgasm hitting the end of the condom and his groans bring on such

49

an intense orgasm that it makes me squirt all over Sir. I hear him yell "YES" just before I pass out.

I wake in the morning to a note that says "My Kitten I NEED MORE, but I had to go home. Call me, and we can set aside more play time."

I flop back onto the bed and smile at the ceiling. Last night was so incredible that I am sated even after eight hours of sleep.

My Friend's Special Visit

I am sitting in my bedroom; I have just turned on my computer since arriving home from work. My friend, Luna called me and told me she was coming over. She said she had something that she wanted to tell me.

Since Luna is coming over it means I need to make sure I am primped and smelling nice. I know she is my friend but she is gorgeous. She has deep chocolate eyes and long black hair.

Her body is made for a man, it's curvy in all the right places and her breasts are huge. I could use them as fluffy pillows.

I have about an hour before she arrives it's time to get pumped and primped. I jump into the shower.

Erotic Bedtime Stories

It only takes about 20 minutes in the shower, but I am clean and I have shaved my face and around my cock. I have brushed my hair and lathered on cologne. I have picked out my favorite pair of jeans and a black top, but I am not going to get dressed yet, I have one more thing I need to attend to and it's pointing straight ahead.

I walk over to me computer and sit down. I need a little inspiration; I search through my favorite porn site and pick the one I want. It just happens to be friends fucking. My cock instantly turns rock hard and my hand starts a slow pace. I know I am going to have to speed up; I only have about 30 minutes to bust a nut and get dressed before she gets here.

I have just started speeding up my hand; I can feel the tingling low in my stomach. My balls are drawing up and the urge to come is urgent. I pick up speed and within second I have come all over my stomach. I have to close my eyes and catch my breath. I come back from the orgasm I just had and look at the clock. I have 10 minutes to get cleaned up and get dressed, so I rush to the bathroom.

I have just stepped out of my room when I hear a knock on my door. I walk to my door and look through the peephole. She is wearing a low-cut top that make her breast stand out, she is just about to knock again when I swing open the door. I can feel my cock stir in my pants and pray that I will be able to fight off the impending hard on long enough for her to tell me what she needs to and then leave.

She looks at me and tells me "It's about damn time you opened the door, I have been standing out her forever." Then she giggles and walks into my apartment.

I reach for her to give her a hug, while also trying to hide the semi in my pants and welcome her. I haven't seen her in about two months; she has been off in the Middle East, doing something for her job.

"Hey Lue, how have you been?" I ask her and step away.

I spin away from her and adjust myself to find the right comfort for my cock. These damn pants are too tight. I didn't realize she walked behind me until I feel her hand on my ass; I jerk my head around and look into her eyes. She has a small smile on her face, and she steps closer so that her tits press into my chest. "Did you miss me Dom?" she whispers and runs her hand through my hair.

I groan but ask her "What are you doing Lue?" and place my hands loosely on her hips while pulling her closer to me.

"You know Dom, I missed seeing you for the two months I was away, and do you know what I need?" She whispers into my ear, and then she runs her tongue down my neck and bites my shoulder.

"Are you sure you want this Lue? If you are then you need to lock my door and take everything off." I tell her in a low voice and look into her eyes. Those chocolate orbs are locked on my black ones, and she nods and steps towards the door.

Erotic Bedtime Stories

I turn to get myself gathered together, when I hear the lock click on the door. I turn and see her shirt hit the floor and I bear witness to the sexiest strip tease I have ever seen. The sway of her hips has me hypnotized and the bounce of her breast has my cock standing at full attention, which makes my jeans that, much more uncomfortable.

By the time she makes it back to me she is completely naked, and she drops to her knees in front of me. Her head is bowed, and she is waiting to be told what to do. "Luna, do you want my cock?" I ask. She nods her head and I tell her "With words Luna". "Yes, Dom I need your cock" she whispers. I start to undo my pants and let them slide to the floor. "Eyes up Luna and take my cock in your mouth" I demand.

Her head snaps up, and she looks straight at my cock, she slowly runs her hands up my legs and sends an electric current through my system that makes my already stiff cock bounce. Before I can sit down she has engulfed my cock to the hilt with her warm wet mouth. She sets a pace that is quick and her sucking has so much force that it feels like she has reached inside me and pulled my orgasm from out of nowhere. I don't have time to warn her before I shoot my load down her throat and groan from the release and fall to the couch.

She chuckles as she stands and immediately I grab her hips and bring her close. I latch on to the perfectly round tit that is right in front of my face and suck the brown peaked nipple into my mouth which has her moaning.

I slowly stand and walk her back towards my bed and gently push her so that she falls on the bed. When she lands the bounce of her breast make me groan, and then she spreads her legs. Her glistening pussy is on full display for my eyes and it makes my mouth water.

It's her turn to come, so I slowly prowl up the bed, between her spread legs and start to place kisses and nips up her

Erotic Bedtime Stories

inner thighs. I have come to the part where I get to drive my tongue into her honey pot, but instead I use my teeth and gently bite down on her throbbing clit causing her to arch of the bed and moan loud. "Babe, if you want me to continue you're going to have to be quiet. Grab a pillow and bite down." I whisper to her and watch as she grabs for a pair of clean socks and sticks them in her mouth. I bite her clit again and flick my tongue over the hard numb and then run my tongue stiffly down her center. I have her squirming and moaning and I can feel her start to pulse when I insert my finger into her heat and curve so that I can rub her g spot.

I have just started my first circle on her g spot when I latch onto her clit and suck hard causing her to squeeze my finger in her tight pussy and come so hard I can hear her gasping for breath.

I release my mouth from her clit but continue to rub and pump my finger in and out of her driving her into another orgasm.

I remove my finger and stand to get my condom on when I notice that she has flipped over on all four and has her as in the air. I grab the foil packet and walk to my computer and put a mellow song on. I rip open the foil and roll the condom over my stiff cock.

I tell her to come closer to the edge of the bed and as she gets into position I slam my full length inside her. I don't give her time to adjust; I am too far gone and just need to release all my frustrations. My pace is quick and hard. I bring my hand down hard twice on her ass and hear her moan around the sock.

I feel her pussy gripping at me with each thrust and it causes me to slam inside her and still. My cock lengthens and my come jets out of me hitting the condom with such strength that I swear I ripped a hole in it, which causes her to splinter and squirt her juices all over me. I smile because she has been the only girl I have ever been able to do that with and it feels fan-fucking-tastic.

Erotic Bedtime Stories

I pull out of her and look at my condom, still intact no holes. I breathe a sigh of relief. I walk into my bathroom and clean myself off. By the time I come back out, Luna has gotten fully dressed and standing at the door. What she says next hurts, but I know it's true.

"We can never do this again; I came to tell you that I am getting married and moving back to the Middle East with my husband!!" Then she leaves. I go to my computer turn off the music and get back to playing my game. I am just getting my brain back into the game when my friend messages me and asks to hang out. I think why the heck not, get away from what just happened.

I am not embarrassed in the least and when I strut out of my apartment and see Lela standing by the elevator waiting to go down. The look on her face has me smirking. She wants me again, yet she is the one that said she can't. So, I send her a wink and adjust my cock in my pants and walk down the stairs.

Erotic Bedtime Stories

A Workout for Him

I've been in this exercise class for three weeks now. It's mainly all woman and a few men, whose sole purpose in the class is to check out the women when they bend over and the bounce of their chest when they jump.

Today I happened to be placed in front of a large window. It allows other patrons of the gym to see the classes that are in session, but it also allows the men who aren't stupid enough to join the class to watch the women in the class.

Normally I hide in the back of the class, but I was running late today, so I'm stuck right in front of the window. I'll just tune out and focus on the instructor.

We are about half-way through the class when I get the feeling like I am being watched. I bend to take a sip of my water, and out of the corner of my eye I see a man, and he has his eyes firmly planted on my body, and they are following my every move. He stands about six foot two and has brown hair and is absolutely gorgeous.

I stand up and stretch with my arms above my head and notice his movements, his hand reaches below the glass and that is all I can see, I turn back to the instructor to finish off the rest of the class,

Once the class has finished I head to the locker room. I need to have a shower and get dressed. I have to go to the grocery store then head home.

I am just heading out the front door when the receptionist yells "MISS" and rounds the counter heading for me. Standing there wondering if I am in trouble or not. She reaches me and hands me a note and then turns around and walks back to her desk.

Looking at the note in my hand, I turn and start to walk towards my car. I will read it when I get to my car.

Erotic Bedtime Stories

As I reach my car I notice another note on my windshield, what the hell is going on. I take the note off and look at it; all it ends up being is an advertisement for a sex club in downtown. I throw it in my backseat with my gym bag and get behind the wheel.

Before I start the car, I look at the note that the receptionist handed to me. Written in a messy cursive is: Beautiful, Meet me for dinner at 7:00pm tonight at Sacraphina's. Be there or I WILL find you!

I chuckle to myself and throw the note on the passenger seat. I think to myself sure I'll meet a stranger at a restaurant that is half an hour away from my home, for all I know he could be a psycho with bigger issues that I don't know about.

I start the car and head to the grocery store.

It's seven o'clock and I have just finished watching my favorite cooking show, when I hear the doorbell ring. It's probably my next-door neighbor's daughter selling chocolates for school. I grab my wallet on the way to the door and swing it open with a smile on my face. The smile on my face dies when I stare into the deepest green eyes I've ever seen. My mouth hangs open because it's the guy from the gym. He looks angry and his eyes show a mixed emotion of lust and anger.

"You were supposed to meet me at Sacraphina's. Why are we here standing in your doorway and not sitting at a candlelight dinner sipping wine? I had the perfect night planned, first dinner and then a night of pleasure. Why are you here in a tight pair of yoga pants and a tank top watching cooking shows?" He rants.

I just stare at him with my mouth hanging open; my eyes are locked on his. He steps closer to me and reaches out his arm. His hand cups my chin, and he murmurs "My Beautiful".

I snap out of my trans and whisper "How did you find me?"

Erotic Bedtime Stories

"My Beautiful, I own the gym. I have been waiting to meet you for months, but you always hide." He says.

"I'm just about to stretch out before I head to bed, please leave" I demand, or, so I think. It comes out more like a whimper.

He groans and then states a firm "NO". I open my mouth to tell him off, and he continues. "I am going to watch My Beauty stretch that beautiful body and then you are going to let me play. I've been rock hard for you since I saw you leave this afternoon", and to prove his point he slowly runs his hand down my arm to my wrist where he grabs it and brings it towards his crotch.

"That's all for you, but you are going to have to work for it Beautiful" he whispers and then slams his mouth down on mine.

He slowly pulls his mouth away and says, "Now go stretch, I want to see what your body and bend too."

Erotic Bedtime Stories

I stare at him and then nod my head
and turn away from him. I hear him groan
and as I look over my shoulder I see his
eyes are glued firmly on my ass. I wiggle it
a little and hear him growl before he says
"STOP! Beautiful, stay where you are, I am
going to run out to my car to get
something, don't move an inch." Then he
turns and walks out of my front door.

He returns minutes later with a
duffle bag, which he sets on the floor by
my stairs, and walks towards my couch.
Then he demands "STRETCH!" as he sits
down.

I roll my eyes and go to my mat.

I am just getting into my first
position and am silently counting to
twenty in my head when he groans and
demands "take off your shirt". I hesitate
and look towards the couch. "Do as I say
Beautiful" he says, he has fire in his eyes
and a huge bulge in his pants.

I get up on my knees and take my
tank top off. I throw it towards him and as
it flies through the air he grabs it and

brings it to his nose and takes a deep breath.

I have been stretching for ten minutes and am in my final pose when I see him move from the couch and casually walk up behind me. As he reaches me he grabs my hips and rubs his erection against my ass and then moans. "Stay exactly like this for me" he whispers and then walks towards the stairs.

I am still in the downward facing dog pose when I feel leather cuffs wrap around my ankles. I look between my legs into his eyes and see that his eyes are glued to my covered crotch, then he whispers, "How much do you like these pants?"

"I have a bunch of them, why" I question? He doesn't answer me just takes out a pocket knife and cuts the inseam of my pants from ankle to ankle.

"Beautiful, you are not wearing any panties?" he growls at me, then starts kissing up my left leg to my knee and then switches to my right at the knee and continues up my thigh, where he starts to nip and lick. Just as he reaches my wet pussy, he inhales a deep breath and growls.

His hand reaches up and I think he is going to sink one finger inside me, but all he does is lightly run his finger around the lips which causes my spine to tingle and then suddenly he slams his tongue deep into my wet and waiting pussy, causing me to moan. He then drags his tongue through my wetness up to my clit where he makes it into a point and flicks his tongue hard on my clit, gasping out "OH GOD" and then moaning I start to shake. His mouth latches onto my clit sucking it deep into his mouth and it makes me come so hard that I see stars and my knees give out.

As my vision clears and I see that I am falling to the floor I try to move my hands to catch myself when my Mystery Man catches me and chuckles "That's one of many, before this night is through you will have come so many times that you will be begging me to stop."

As he places me back on my feet with my ass in the air and my hands on the floor, then I hear him start to undo his pants.

Looking between my legs I see his muscular one's step behind me, and then he slams his cock deep inside me, just as I yell out "CONDOM!"

He is pounding away inside me and I can't fight the impending orgasm that crashes through me just as my Mystery Man pulls out of me. He bends down and undoes the cuffs and carries me to the arm of my couch.

He places me so that I am leaning over the arm and lines himself up, slamming his cock back inside me. He reaches his hand around and pinches my clit. The pain from the pinch and the pleasure from his cock moving inside me causes me to splinter into a mind-blowing orgasm around him.

He pulls out and stands me up then walks over to the couch. He lies down and then demands "ON TOP, I want your pussy on my face and your lips wrapped around my cock". I walk over to him, just getting into position when he grips my hips and brings me down on his tongue, causing me to moan loudly and arch my back.

He reaches his hand up to my neck and pushes my head down onto his glistening cock.

I wrap my lips around his head and start the same intense sucking that he is doing to my clit, causing him to moan into me. He increases the suction on my clit and inserts a finger in a hook, hitting my g spot. This causes his cock to slip from my mouth as I come hard again.

I am slowly catching my breath when I am lifted off of him, and he swings me around so that I am now hovering over his cock.

Pushing into me slowly he sets a steady pace, his lust filled eyes are staring into me as he slides in and out of me over and over again, his thrusts are becoming harder and hitting in the spot deep inside me that cause a mixture of pleasure and pain, but also brings on another orgasm. This one leaves me breathless and feeling like I am jelly.

He is still pounding away, when I cry out, "NO MORE PLEASE!" and collapse on top of him. He doesn't hear me as his groans have become over powering then his thrust increase, I feel his cock lengthen and then I feel hot jets of his come coating my insides causing another orgasm to crash through me and then everything goes black.

When I woke the morning after that I remembered my Mystery Man and the intimate time we had, but I completely forgot that he didn't use a condom, now here I am twelve weeks later, sitting in my OB GYN's office waiting to hear results from a pregnancy test. My legs are bouncing because I am so nervous, when

Erotic Bedtime Stories

the Doctor walks in and says
"Congratulations, your pregnant!"

My Injured Man

I have been stressed for weeks now; about two weeks ago my Dom was injured while doing something he loved. He has been at home in his cast for a week and is bored.

I hope that my little present that I have for him will bring a smile to his face.

As I walk to the door I can hear him breathing hard and I hear moaning, but it's that overly fake porn star moan, so I know he is watching porn on TV. I hope this little present I have under my robe will bring him out of his funk.

I quietly open the door and watch what he is doing. He has one hand firmly gripped on his rock-hard erection and his movements are slow and steady. His eyes are glued to the scene being played out on the T.V.

Erotic Bedtime Stories

"More, Harder, faster" the fake big
boobed woman moans, and she does the
whole arch of her back and throw back of
her head. You can tell the whole video is
fake; I'd actually be shocked if she has an
orgasm.

I turn my attention back to my Dom
and watch as his eyes close. I am so
turned on that I reach into my panties and
start short small circles around my clit,
the pleasure is building in the pit of my
stomach and my hand starts to rub
harder when I hear.

"If you come on your fingers I will
make your ass burn red from my hand" he
demands.

My eyes snap to his, and he is
sitting there staring and my hand in my
panties. I hesitate and smile at him as I
untie my robe and slowly let it fall to the
floor. I hear his breath catch and I look to
the floor.

I have put on my collar with his
initials on it, my black leather corset with
my black leather thong panties and my

74

thigh high stiletto leather boots. My hair is up in two ponytails that flow down the side of my head and my head is bent towards the floor.

I hear him groan and horsley say, "Come here Kitten" and then point to a spot between his legs. Even though his one leg is in cast he was able to spread them wide enough that I fit perfectly in between.

"Look at me Kitten." he whispers and my head snaps up and I stare into his lust filled eyes.

"Did you do this for me?" he says and runs his thumb along my bottom lip. I nod my head.

"No Kitten, use your words, let me hear that sexy voice" he demands.

"Yes Sir, I did this for you, to make you happy, to please you" I say firmly, locking my eyes into his.

He groans and runs his finger down the center of my face dipping into my mouth and then withdrawing it and continuing down between my breasts.

"Straddle me Kitten" he whispers. I comply and place my thighs beside his hips and run my hands down his face.

"Put your hands on the back of the couch Kitten, and don't let go" he demands.

I place my hands on the back of the couch and watch as his head lowers to the bulge of my boobs and runs his tongue over each breast. His hand grabs the zipper on the corset and slowly lowers it expose my full breast.

He moans and takes one nipple into his mouth and sucks then release and flicks his tongue steadily over the nipple causing me to moan and whimper. He switches to the other and repeats the sucking and flicking.

He finally has the corset off and throws it behind the couch. He then uses his hand to slide down and touches my covered pussy and rubs gently.

"This pussy is mine, you touch it again and you will not come for a week. I will take all my pleasure and leave you wanting." He growls.

"Yes Sir" I whimper as his hand rubs harder.

He removes his hand from my covered pussy and I hear a snap as the confines of my leather thong is torn from my body.

"You will not come, your orgasm is mine, and I will take mine before you get yours" he states firmly and then his hand slides between my pussy lips, and he taps my clit repeatedly, causing me to jerk in his arms and moan loudly. His assault on my click is causing a burning need to come, but I have to fight it my pleasure is his to have. The steady strum stops on my clit, and he quickly inserts two fingers and starts a slow steady pace of in and out. I can hear how wet he is making me and see his body growing tighter with the need to release.

Within seconds of him pulling out of me he slides his cock inside me and stills.

"Oh Kitten, you are always so tight and ready for me" he moans, which makes my insides quiver.

He is still firmly planted inside me and his fingers are pinching my nipples, his mouth is sucking on my neck, and then he sinks his teeth into my shoulder as he pulls out of me and slams back in only to still again.

"Kitten I need you stand for me please," he says as he looks into my lazy eyes.

Without saying anything I stand up and wait for his instructions.

His eyes follow the curve of my leg as his hands trace over the same place that his eyes just were. He gets to the top of my boot and slowly slides the zipper down then taps my ankle to make me lift. He throws the boot behind the couch and does the same with the other one. With my boots off I don't have to kneel over his face. He smirks up at me and latches his mouth onto my clit and sucks, causing me to scream out and see stars.

Erotic Bedtime Stories

He lets go just as I am about to come and leaves me while his hands slide up and down my legs. The tension is starting to leave my body from the near orgasm when he latches on again to my clit and sucks hard bring me right back to the star seeing screaming orgasm to stop again and gently run his hands up and down my leg.

I am shaking and ready to explode and then all of a sudden, the urge goes away and I catch my breath for him to latch on again and suck and flick and bring me right back to the urge then stops and taps my legs and tells me "Kneel on the floor Kitten".

I get on the floor and kneel between his legs and look into his eyes.

"Take my cock into your mouth Kitten" he demands and then watches me as I open my mouth and lower it over his swollen head. I continue down his shaft as I hallow out my cheeks, causing him to moan and grab my ponytails.

I have just taken him into my throat deep when he growls "STOP!"

I lift my eyes and feel him pull my hair up, and he pops out of my mouth.

"Ride my cock Kitten, make me come" he states and pulls me into his lap.

He grips my hips and slams me down on his steel erection. He sets a hard pounding pace. He is going to leave bruises on my hips but I don't care.

"Yes Kitten, so fucking tight" he growls and then his pace picks up, his thrusts are hard and deep his motion is fast and demanding, and then all of a sudden he slams me down on his cock and hot jets of come coat the inside of my walls, and then he demands "COME NOW KITTEN!"

I scream out and clench around him as my orgasm rips through me causing me to fall on top of him. My body feels like Jell-O and my breathing is short and fast.

"Thank you, Kitten, now go clean up and get me a cloth" he whispers as he taps my leg to get off of him.

Erotic Bedtime Stories

I walk into the bathroom and feel the slide of his orgasm run down the inside of me, I smile at myself in the mirror and clean up.

I get a warm wash cloth and bring it to him to see that he has passed out. I clean him up and cover him with a throw blanket. I make sure that his pills and a bottle of water are sitting beside him as I head to the shower.

From the Net to Your Bed

I've been chatting with this man for a few weeks now. We meet on a chat page and have been talking to each other every day. He is funny and sympathetic and has enjoyed a few of my jokes. I can be myself with him.

I am staring at his last message sent to me; he has asked to meet me in person. I really like him; do I give in and allow him to meet me or do I say no. I have stared at his message now for five minutes, so I do the next thing and click on my message bar. I want to tell him "I'm not sure; I am nervous" what I do write is "Yeah sure, where and when?"

"Tonight, at seven I will meet you at Chez Maya, wear a royal blue dress" he sends and then you see him disconnect from the chat bubble.

Erotic Bedtime Stories

It is six forty-five, and I am sitting in my car in the parking lot of Chez Maya. I have been working up the nerve to go into the restaurant for the last five minutes. I see a car pull up that is absolutely stunning. It's midnight blue and sporty the person in the car must have some money for something so sleek. A man gets out of the car, he is wearing a gray suit and his hair is short that is all I can see from here. His back and butt are tight by the looks, and he walks with a swagger that says, "I'm important move out of the way".

I decide to go and see if Dominick has even shown up, with my luck he is not even thinking about me.

I walk into the front of the restaurant and approach the hostess. "I am here to meet someone, but I don't know his last name." I whisper to the girls. She looks at me and then looks down to me dress and says, "Ah there you are, follow me Mr. Moore has been waiting for you to arrive", and points me towards a section of the restaurant that is all sectioned into closed off areas. At the moment only one section is wide open, so I ask, "The one with the door open?" She nods curtly and turned back to face the front. This allows me to catch my breath and walk towards the open door.

As I enter the door I notice that there is nobody in the area, but I notice and single red rose on the table and a card folded in half. I pick up the card and read My Beautiful Callie, please remove your panties and place them on the plate on the table in front of the empty seat and then sit down; I will be with you momentarily.

I sigh and sit down; I am wearing my string pair of panties, so I don't take them off. I close my eyes and take a deep breath. Then I hear whispered in a deep voice "I told you to put your panties on my plate, do it now or you will earn a whip of my belt."

My eyes snap open and my breath stills as I stare into the brown eyes of Dominick. I know this is Dominick because he has sent me a picture and his eyes are glowing with lust.

I slowly stand from my chair and reach under my dress. I hook my fingers into the string at the side and pull the bow causing the panties to fall to the floor.

With my eyes, still on his I bend down to pick them up.

He growls and whispers "Stay like that but open your legs wide".

I do as he says and the rumble that comes from his throat is erotic. It sends electric pulses to my pussy and makes my juices start to flow.

I see him take a deep breath and then says, "Do I turn you on Callie?" I nod my head.

He walks towards the sliding doors and closes them, I hear the lock click into place, and then he clicks a button which makes the windows tint a deep shade. "No worries Callie, no one can see your sexy body but me" he whispers into the room.

I shiver at his words and start to stand.

"When you stand I want you completely naked." He demands.

I stand tall and start to undo my zipper at the side of my dress and slowly let the dress fall to floor. I couldn't wear a bra as the dress I had was strapless so it leaves me in nothing but my platform stilettos.

"Sit please Callie, let's enjoy dinner" He says and I flash him a panicked look.

He chuckles and then says "Relax Sweetness, the restaurant has already placed our food in the room. No one will be viewing your delectable body, but me."

I relax into my seat and enjoy the view of the man sitting in front of me. His eyes are burning with lust and I can tell he is starting to get hot; by the way he is adjusting his neck tie and swallowing repeatedly.

"Now Sweetness, I need you to stand and come to me." He whispered in a husky voice while motioning with his finger in a "come here" motion.

Erotic Bedtime Stories

I stand from my chair and walk to just beside him. He doesn't look at me; he just moves his dinner setting to where mine is and croaks out "lie down on the table please."

My eyes flash to his and I sit down and swing my legs so that they dangle off the table and lie back. I slowly close my eyes until I hear him groan, and he grabs my hand, and places it on his rock-hard erection.

He stands and walks over to the tray that I just noticed in the room. He lifts the lid and I can smell an array of scents.

"This is an appetizer tray. I am going to place these on your body and eat them off your gorgeous skin." He states as he walks towards me with the tray.

He strategically places the appetizer on my body in places that when his mouth hits will send a jolt of pleasure spiraling throughout my body.

As he finishes placing all the items, his stomach growls, and he begins. He grabs the watermelon he placed on my neck and drags it from ear to ear and then places the piece on my lips. He then starts at my right ear and runs his tongue along my neck the same way that he did with the watermelon and brings his lips to mine where he takes a bite of the watermelon then proceeds to push the rest of the watermelon into my mouth with his tongue as he kisses me.

He lifts his head and whispers "delicious" and then smiles.

He heads to my right breast and the cheese he had placed on both nipples, he runs his tongue around the cheese and then sucks taking the cheese and my nipple into his mouth where he lightly bites down and then flicks his tongue on the hard nipple. He repeats the process on the other nipple this time bringing the cheese to my lips and pushing it into my mouth with his tongue. He follows this up with another groan.

My body is humming with anticipation and need, I can feel the slow burn in the pit of my stomach and the urgent need to cum is making me squirm on the table.

"Stay still Sweetness, I'm going to take my time for this next part. I want you to hold onto your orgasm until I tell you too, do you understand?" he asks me. I nod my head and whisper "yes".

He smiles and positions himself between legs. He had placed some cut up strawberries across my pelvis; he then throws my legs over his shoulders and licks up the inside of my thigh to the first strawberry. He grabs it between his teeth and drags the tip down through my slit and positions it so that is in between my folds at my opening. Then he runs his tongue back up my folds to get the next strawberry, he does this until all the slices are placed in my folds. There are four slices placed in me and a very throbbing clit waiting for his lips to suck it into his mouth.

He pauses a second to look up into my eyes. His eyes are glowing with lust; I'm assuming that my eyes are a mirror image of his. He smiles and then I watch his head descend between wide spread thighs.

He sucks my throbbing clit back into his mouth and flicks his tongue at a steady pace over and over until he feels my hips start to grind on his face. He then lifts his head and moves to the first strawberry and runs his tongue in between my folds to flick the strawberry into his mouth.

On the second strawberry, he does the same but this time he brings his mouth up to mine and slams his lips down on them, while using his tongue to push the strawberry into my mouth.

He heads down to the fourth strawberry leaving the third one still inside me. When he pushes his tongue under the strawberry it enters into me, where he mimics the in and out motion and then sucks the strawberry into his mouth.

My nerves are on edge. I need to cum; like I need to drink water, but every time my hips meet his face to get more friction he pulls away and kisses the inside of my thigh.

The third strawberry instead of using his tongue he uses his fingers to pluck it out and places it in between his lips, he then inserts two fingers into me and starts a slow pace of in and out.

As his fingers are working my body into a huge ball of energy that needs to release, he brings his lips to mine and pushes the strawberry into my mouth. I quickly chew and swallow it and open my mouth for him while his tongue mimics what his fingers are doing.

"Sweetness, I can feel your cunt tightening on my fingers, cum for me." He whispers in my ear, causing me to moan low and allow my orgasm to crash through me.

I am still in the middle of my orgasm when his fingers are pulled from me and I hear him remove his clothing and then before I can come back down he slams his full length inside me and groans "so fucking tight".

He doesn't say anything after that, all you can hear in the room is his grunts and groans, my moans and whimpers. He brings me to two more orgasms before he pulls out and flips me over.

I am now bent over the table and panting when he eases back into me and slows his strokes.

"Sweetness, you are mine. Your body will be for my eyes only, your pussy will be filled with my cum, and mine alone, you will not let anyone else touch it." He groans and then picks up his pounding pace.

I am on the verge of my fourth orgasm when his pace starts to falter and his grip gets tighter on my hips then he slams in causing my orgasm to crash through causing me to squirt all over his cock as he lengthens and then drops his head back on a moan, and he spills is cum inside me.

"That was the fucking hottest sex I have ever had. Next time will be at my place and I will be inside you all night and the following day. Get dressed Sweetness I will drive you home." He says then pulls out of me and uses his hand to push his cum back into my body. I look at him confused at what he is doing; he smiles and shrugs his shoulders. He helps me stand up and then hands me my dress.

It takes us five minutes to get fully dressed and heading out the door. He wouldn't let me have my panties back said he needed a souvenir of when he finally met the woman who had his mind and body. He also informed me that his heart was already fighting his body to have her again.

He drops me off at my house, and before I leave the car he leans over and gives me a kiss then proceeds to tell me "I will see you tomorrow Sweetness. I'll talk to you when I get home."

I get out of the car and float up to my apartment. I make it into my bedroom and flop down on my bed. It takes mere seconds for me to blissfully fall asleep.

I wake up in the morning to a chat message from Dominick:

"Sweetness, it looks like I tired you out. Just thought I'd let you know that if you should become pregnant we will be married as soon as you tell me. You are mine, and I will be giving you my name in the future or sooner if you are with child. Love you! D"

Voyeur Roommates

To say that the house I rent a room in is nice would be an understatement. I have lived in this house for the last year. My roommates are fantastic. We all get along and are more like best friends than anything else.

Although I do have to admit that Travis is the tall, dark extremely handsome with a side of mysterious. He has long dark hair that he keeps tied back and his eyes are like looking into the black abyss, but his body is chiseled and damn the man can take my breath away with the flex of a muscle.

Then you have Jacob, he is your typical surfer boy, shaggy blonde hair, crystal blue eyes, a nice golden tan and the odd scar on his legs from bashing them off the surfboard.

Trina is the blonde bombshell. She is an utter bitch to the people she doesn't like and has a face that is constantly set to looking like she swallowed a bunch of sour candy.

Me I am Jess. I am curvy and shy. Brown hair curls around my face and my dusty gray eyes are wide and welcoming. I am a total nerd and love everything that makes me think. I will go out of my way to help one of my roommates even if they usually don't reciprocate.

I am just getting ready to head into the shower when I hear the front door close. This sound means I am alone in the house, so I slide into the shower and prepare for my ultimate shower fantasy.

Every time I am in the shower alone I always fantasize about Travis sliding into the shower with me. While we are in the shower he licks and sucks his way up and down my body making me orgasm with his tongue and fingers, before he slides his rock-hard erection swiftly into my wet body.

Erotic Bedtime Stories

Usually during this fantasy, I will use my fingers to rub slow circles around my tighten clit and then slowly slide my fingers down and insert them quickly making the wet suction noise with my fingers causing me to moan loudly and shutter when my orgasm rips through my body.

Just as I am finishing off my shower I hear a low groan and then a loud thud. I wonder if it is our next door neighbors. Usually we hear their every move, but I could swear I heard them leave this morning already.

Wrapping the towel around my body I head out of the bathroom heading towards my bedroom when I see Travis door open a touch. It's open enough that I can see into his bed. He is standing in his room with his pants around his ankles. He is on the phone but his one hand is slowly moving back and forth. He turns slightly to the side and I get the full picture of what he is doing.

He has his hand wrapped around his cock and is slowly moving it up and down his shaft. He is a big man but his cock is huge. I hear him say to whoever he is talking to "Get here now I need those red lips wrapped around my cock."

I look down at the floor and walk back to my room. Closing the door I flop down onto the bed and stare at the ceiling.

Slowly coming out of my depression over not being able to bed Travis I get dress and head to the kitchen.

Passing Travis' room just as he roars "Yes Jess, take it all".

I think to myself that he must have another girl in there with him named Jess. I head into the kitchen and make myself a cup of tea and a slice of toast.

Travis and a skinny brunette come walking out to the kitchen fifteen minutes later. The brunette looks at me and smiles then whispers something into Travis ear. His eyes flash to hers, and then he grunts in the affirmative.

Erotic Bedtime Stories

She smiles at me and then taps
Travis' crotch and walks out the door.

I shake my head and go to the
couch.

Everybody has been home now for
an hour. Jacob and Trina are making out
on the couch. His hand is sliding up her
thighs and back down. Trina stops to take
a breath and then says, "your room now"
and jumps off his lap.

I quietly sneak down the hall and
watch through his door. He is lying on his
back on the bed her legs are straddling his
head and his face is buried in her pussy,
whatever he is doing is causing her to
moan around the head of his cock, which
in turn causes him to groan.

I run my hand around my boobs
and pinch my nipples causing me to gasp.
Just as I am reaching for the other nipple
Trina's back arches and she yells out "Yes
baby, Yes" and then her body starts to
shake.

Jacob quickly lifts her of his face
and reaches in the drawer beside his bed

and pulls out a roll of condoms. He tears into one and rolls it over his erection and then demands Trina to "ride his cock".

Letting my hands slow drift down my pants and into my panties I quietly listen to Jacob and Trina fucking each other. This isn't the first time that they have had sex or that I have watched. It's a total turn on to watch others have sex.

I have just started to put pressure onto my hardened clit and make slow circles around, fighting the moan as the pleasure builds in my stomach.

I smell Travis before I feel him against my back. I start to bring my hands out from my pants when he stops me by gripping my wrist.

"Don't Jess, keep playing with your pussy, your smell is driving me insane" he whispers in my ear.

My eye's flash to his as his lips descend on my neck, and he says against it "I want you Jess, I need to have that sweet-smelling pussy wrapped around my cock milking all my cum."

100

My breath hitches as he guides me to his bedroom.

"Clothes off Jess and lie on my bed" he states.

"No Travis, I am not having sex with you after the other girl was here earlier for it" I say and walk out of his room into my own swinging the door closed behind me.

I climb under my covers and completely ignore the burning need to cum. I am just falling to sleep when I hear my door open and then my covers are moved back and Travis slides in behind me.

I have been lying beside Travis for half an hour now and every minute he slides some part of his body closer to mine.

"Jess?" Travis whispers.

"What Travis?" I answer.

"I have a confession to make but I want you to hear me out fully, before you answer ok" He states getting up on his elbow and rolling me to face him.

"I have a lot to tell you but I want to say this first and foremost, you are my every thought." He starts as I flash him my "Yeah ok" face.

"Just listen, Yes I had a woman in my room, no I did not have sex with her. I let her suck my cock, while I pictured you. I was listening at the bathroom door, while you were flicking your clit. I listen to you moan my name, and while you were doing that I had my hand wrapped around my cock. I had to call Mandie because I couldn't face you for dinner while I had a lead pipe in my pants." He takes a deep breath.

He looks down into my eyes as his hand glides up to the hem of my shirt, slowly he guides it up and lets his finger trail along my skin causing me to break out in goose bumps. He brings the shirt up over my head and stops at my elbows. He then grabs my right wrist and crosses over to my left elbow and tuck it into the shirt, doing the same with my left wrist.

His lust filled eyes follow the curve of my body as he takes in my upper half. His eyes linger on my boobs causing him to lick his lips and moan.

He gets up onto his knees and his hands go to my PJ bottoms. He slowly slides them down my legs letting out a groan when he sees that I have no panties on underneath my sleep pants. The pants are left hanging off of my left ankle.

He then gets off the bed and wraps the pants tighter and secures them to the leg of my bedpost. Then he grabs my sheet and wraps it around the other leg and secures that to the other leg, leaving my legs spread.

His cock is standing proud and pointing up his eyes are scanning my legs as he bends down and places a soft kiss on my left ankle and then on my right.

He moves slowly up my legs placing soft kisses up both legs. The closer he gets to my pussy the more excited I get. My body is tingling I can feel a slow build in my stomach and the anticipation of my throbbing clit.

He is in between my legs; he hasn't said anything or touch my pussy. He places kisses all around my pubic area, but has yet to sample my wetness.

His eyes connect with mine and his head deeps as he softly kisses my clit, slowly sliding his tongue out in a point and flicking it, causing my back to arch and my head to drop back and a slow moan to slide from my mouth.

He continues his slow sensuous attack of my pussy, sliding his tongue in and down, sucking and nipping slowly building my orgasm to a peek. I start to moan and chant his name when he demands "NO SOUNDS" and sucks my click hard into his mouth.

The sudden suction causes my orgasm to crash through my body and I suck in a big deep breath and hold it, causing my eyes to cross and I start to see stars slowly blacking out. "Jess, breath for me baby" I hear Travis voice making me let release the breath that I was holding.

My heart is pounding, my chest is heaving and my breaths are coming in quickly and in shorts spurts. Taking a big deep breath and release it.

I hear Travis chuckle from between my legs and then two fingers are pushed inside me and hooked the longest one up to rub my g-spot. Bring the orgasm I just finished racing back into my body and crashing over the edge. This time I remember to breathe through it, but I don't remember to stay quiet as I moan.

Travis prowls up my body and places his lips on mine, he whispers "For the noise, while I fuck you. You can't cum; once I have had my orgasm pimped into your tight body I will tell you to cum." Then he places his uncovered cock at my opening and slowly slides in. My eyes flash to his face, I see that his head is tossed back, and he is groaning as his body pumped into mine.

"So, fucking tight, so fucking hot, so fucking wet and all fucking mine" he groans.

His pace is starting to pick up, my orgasm is starting bloom and his breathing is becoming raged he yells "Jess, baby I need you to cum NOW!"

I splinter around his hard cock and yell "Oh, God! Oh, God! Oh, God! TRAVIS!"

My quaking pussy milks his cock as jets of cum coat my insides.

He collapses on top of me as we both collect ourselves. His head is in my neck and his breathing is tickling as he catches it.

"Jess, I want you to be mine and only mine from now on." He whispers in my ear. I don't say anything just nod as his hands slide up to undo my arms, so I can wrap them around his neck.

We have just started kissing when we hear a soft moan and both our heads snap towards the door.

Standing there with his hands in Trina's pants is Jacob. His eyes are glued to Travis and I and his other hand is working his cock. Just as Trina hits her peak and cums he jerks one last time as his cum coats Trina's side and then the both say "That was fucking hot" before walking out of the room and closing the door.

Travis and I look at each other and start to laugh and then break off as I roll over, and he snuggles into my back and whispers "Good night my girl."

Office Tryst

"Mr. Wilson, you have Ms. Simard on line one for you" I say into the phone.

"Ok Lucy, in five minutes I need you in my office" my boss demands and hangs up the phone.

I have an undeniably large crush on my Boss. He is six feet with well styled brown hair, ocean blue eyes and a smile that lights up a room. He has thick muscular arms and thighs that look perfect for sitting on.

Lost in thought about J.J Wilson my gorgeous Boss, I don't realize that I am rubbing my pussy through my dress pants until I start to feel the tingles in my belly. I am brought out of my intimate daydream fantasies by the buzzing of the phone on my desk.

I reach for the phone and answer "Yes Mr. Wilson?"

"NOW" is all he demands.

I jump out of my seat and gather my laptop up and head to his office door.

As I reach the door I stop and take a deep breath and then push into his office.

"I said five minutes Lucy, I had to call you. Now sit!" He growls as he points to the chair in front of his desk.

He is pushed right into his desk and his elbows are on the desk as I sit down and open my laptop.

"Ok Mr. Wilson, what do you need me for right now" I say while opening up my speech to text document.

"Lucy put your computer away" he says in a husky voice.

My eyes fly to his and see lust and desire pooled there.

"Ok Mr. Wilson" I whisper and close my laptop and put it on the coffee table.

"Luce, please call me JJ" he whispers.

"Ok Mr... I mean JJ, what would you like of me" I say, my voice sounding stronger.

He groans and then makes a come here motion with his finger.

I stand and approach the front of his desk. He shakes his head and then points to a spot on the floor right beside him.

I round the desk and stand in the spot he pointed to.

"Lucy, I need you to take off all your clothes for me" he growls.

"Um excuse me JJ" I question and start to take a step back. His hand flies out and lands on my hip.

"Please kitten, I can't take it anymore I need to see you, I need to feel you" he says quietly as his thumb makes slow sensual circles on my hip and his pleading eyes are begging me to follow his instructions.

I nod slowly and then whisper, "Let me go lock the door."

Erotic Bedtime Stories

He smiles at me and as I turn to go to the door he smacks my ass and then groans.

I slowly walk to the door, putting an extra flare in my step as a show to JJ and lock the door when I reach it.

As I turn my eyes connect with his and I start to unbutton my blouse in an erotic sensually slow strip tease as I walk towards him.

My panties being taken off as I reach the spot where he told me to stand, as I go to throw them behind me his one hand grabs my wrist and his other hand reaches for the panties, and he takes them. Bringing them to his nose and inhales then moans.

"Your panties are wet Lucy, who were you thinking of to make your sweet pussy soaked" he asks with a mischievous glint in his eyes.

I lean down and whisper in his ear "You JJ, before you called me in I had my hand on my pussy, and I was day dreaming that you were inside me." This gets me a quick gasp and a deep groan.

"Get your beautiful ass on my desk and put your feet on the arms of my chair" he demands.

I quickly jump on his desk and place my feet on the arms of his chair.

I look down to make sure my feet are on the arms of the chair, I see his pants are open and his hard cock is pointing up with pre cum leaking from the tip.

My eyes jump to his and his are locked onto my clit which is hard and throbbing wanting to be sucked and rubbed.

His hand starts at my ankle and slowly guides up my leg. He has his other hand perch on the arm of the chair with his head resting on it.

Just as his hand on my leg reaches just above my knee his office phone rings. Instead of removing his hand from my leg he reaches out with the other one and answers the phone.

112

"JJ Wilson" he states just as his hand reaches my upper thigh, causing me to whimper.

"Can you hold for a second Marten" he asks then press the hold button.

"Kitten, I have a conference call" he starts to say and I slowly try to get up from his desk, which causes him to place his hand on my pussy and force my body to stop moving.

"You are not going to move from this desk, you need to watch my eyes and my hands, and you need to keep extremely quiet. Do not come until I tell you too" he demands. I nod my head and relax on his desk.

He takes the call off hold and answers "Sorry Marten, where were we?"

He takes the hand on my pussy away and starts to run his middle finger around the lips every so often dipping into my center. I throw my head back and bit the inside of my cheek and just enjoy the feel of his finger.

He has been on the call for fifteen minutes and is still in the process of teasing me slowly when he takes two fingers and pushes them into me, causing me to slap my hand over my mouth and just enjoy the feeling his fingers are doing to me, slowly sliding in and out of my pussy. Bringing my orgasm slowly forward, the orgasm is just at the tingling stage when he hooks his fingers and starts to massage my g spot.

The constant movement of his finger inside me has the orgasm crashing through me and I'm on the verge of going over when he presses a button to mute the phone conversation and then demands "Come Kitten Now!"

This causes me to through my head back and see stars as my body release the most intense orgasm I have hand by anyone with fingers including myself. I am slowly being brought back to earth when I feel his fingers remove from my core, and he leans over so that his face is within my line of vision and inserts his two fingers in his mouth and cleans my release from his fingers.

"Once you catch your breath, I want those perfect pink lips wrapped around my dick. Do not make me come, once I tap you on the head get off and turn around facing my door. Then place your soaked pussy over my cock and just sit. Do you get it" he asks? I nod and smile at him while he sits down and takes the phone off mute.

I remove my legs from the arms of the chair and slowly slide down from his desk to the floor making sure to connect my eyes to his. His eyes go dark, and he follows my every move as I hit the floor with my knees and start to work on loosening his pants. He lifts his ass as I slide down his pants.

Once his pants are on the floor I run my tongue up the inside of his leg and flick my tongue over his balls and up his shaft to the mushroom head of his cock and lick the pre-cum from the top and place a gentle kiss on his pubic bone.

Erotic Bedtime Stories

His breathing has picked up and I
can hear him trying to maintain a
professional composure, while I take this
cock in my mouth and slowly slide down
his shaft allowing his head to hit the back
of my throat and then slide back up.

I set a slow rhythm of up and down
when I feel his hands slide into my hair
and loosen the tight bun allowing my hair
to fall around my face and onto his thighs.

He rubs my hair around his thighs
and I feel him tense, and then he taps my
head as I am taking him deep into my
throat. Slowly coming back up and
hollowing out my cheeks, I let him pop out
of my mouth and start to stand.

As me head comes forward he hooks
me around the back of my neck and pulls
me forward so that our lips crash into
each other, and he slides his tongue into
my mouth just as Marten asks him a
question. Causing him to pause to answer
then licks a line up my jaw to my lips, he
takes my bottom lip in between his teeth
and pulls and releases and then kisses a

line to my ear and whispers "sit on my
cock Kitten."

I nod my head and turn around
slowly sliding my body onto his cock and
still. The feel of his cock stretching me and
filling me makes the walls of my pussy
clench around him causing his head to fall
back against the chair and his grip on my
hips to tighten. I am going to have ten
fingerprint bruises on my hips, but it will
be totally worth it.

He removes his hand quickly from
my hips and presses the mute button,
then groans really loudly and says, "You
feel so fucking good".

"You are going to ride my cock
slowly, so I can finish up this call and
then I take over" he demands and then
uses his arms to show me how slow he
wants me moving. My head falls back and
his falls forward as the bump into each
other.

Slowly moving on top of him, letting
his cock slide in and out of me, fighting

the urge to moan and scream his name as I listen to the end of the call.

"Gentleman thank you for meeting on such short notice. I have something to delve into in thirty seconds, so I am going to hang up. Until the next meeting." He says and then hangs up the phone.

"My turn Kitten, stand up and be prepared to scream" he demands and taps my clit and pushes my forward.

I am bent over his desk, and he slams his cock back into me and starts a pace that has my orgasm rips through my body and squeezes his cock. Hey yells out "Oh Fuck yeah keep going".

I feel wetness hit my back hole, and then he slowly slides a finger into my and starts moving them in and out to the rhythm of his cock in my pussy.

The sensation is so erotic that another orgasm barrels into me and I see stars as I let my head fall onto the desk.

"Kitten I am going to fill you up with my come and then watch it as it leaks out of your pussy. I want to go to lunch with

the knowledge that I am still inside you."
He growls and yells my name as hot
spurts of come coat the inside of me.

He collapses on top of me I feel his
labored breathing and feel his erection
start to weaken.

"You have just rendered me
speechless Lucy, do you know what this
means?" he whispers into the office.

I shake my head and turn to look
over my shoulder into his eyes.

He raises his head and stands up
pulling me up and spinning me around.

"You my Kitten are mine and only
mine, I will be collaring you to show the
world that Lucy Green belongs to JJ
Wilson" He states proudly as he little
kisses my lips.

I smile and whisper against his lips
"Finally", causing him to chuckle.

"Get dressed Luce, it's time for the
world to see that we belong to each other"
he says and pushes me towards the
bathroom to clean up.

Erotic Bedtime Stories

Stay Quiet

I don't know why I told Shay that I'd meet her at the movie theater. I know what's going to happen, she is either not going to show up or she will be with a group of other people and I will be left to sit by myself.

She does this to me every time.

At least I will get to see the newest movie that I have been dying to see.

I have been waiting in the theater now for fifteen minutes, when my phone chimes with a text alert.

Shay: I'm sorry; I have a group of friends with me.

Me: I figured that, every F'n time Shay. WTF I'll sit alone like usual.

I don't give her a chance to respond, I shut my phone down until after the movie is finished.

Just as I set up my spot with my drink in the holder someone sits down beside me. I am right in the middle of the theater and I know to the left of me is an older couple who look cute holding hands and this new person who is sitting now on my right.

I swing my eyes to look directly into the eyes of a perfect stranger who is sitting with a group of guys.

In the minimal light of the theater before the movie starts you can tell that his eyes hold an intensity to them, and his face holds a seriousness to it.

"That's my holder" he growls.

I look down to wear my pop is sitting and then look back at this jerk of a man, instead of starting an argument I remove my cup and place it between my legs and turn to face the front of the theater.

I hear the guys beside me start to whisper and hit each other.

Shaking my head, I turn back just as the movie starts.

Erotic Bedtime Stories

I have been watching the movie for about twenty minutes when I feel, a rough finger run down my arm.

I swing my head and narrow my eyes at the guy sitting beside me, he isn't paying attention, his hand is absently running up and down my arm, so I move my position and turn back to the movie.

I feel his hand hit my thigh closest to him and start drawing figure eights making sure the top loop goes higher each time he comes up.

I slap my hand down on his hand and hiss "What the fuck do you think you are doing?"

He looks at me and smiles then shrugs his shoulders, before he turns his head back to the movie.

I don't know what is going on, but I am thinking about just leaving.

I reach down to grab my stuff when his hand lands on my arm again.

He leans into my body and whispers in my ear, "Please don't leave. My name is Cole and you intrigue me."

His voice and his hand on me send chills through my body, I feel his hand tighten and see his eyes grow heavy with lust.

I smile at him and sit back, return my eyes to the screen and relax.

His body moves closer to me as his arm goes around the behind me, his mouth comes to my ear and his other hand lands on my thigh.

"I have a proposition for you?" Cole whispers into my ear.

I turn my head slightly to listen to what he has to say.

"I want to make you cum on my hand, right here, right now. You have to stay extremely quiet. Once you are done and the movie is done, I want you to meet me in the men's washroom, so I can sink into your tight, wet heat. Are you game?" he whispers into my ear.

I'm so turned on that my brain is sitting with my throbbing clit and I nod my head.

Erotic Bedtime Stories

He moans into my ear, runs his tongue down my neck and bites my pulse point with so much force that I have to cover my mouth to stop the moan.

I didn't dress up to go to the movies, so I am wearing my Capri leggings and loose gym shirt.

He slides his free hand over my chest making sure to pinch my nipples, makes tiny circles on my stomach before he puts his hand in my pants and panties, resting his fingers on my wet pussy lips.

"Turned on, are we? Remember be quiet!" he whispers just as he inserts his middle finger between my folds and taps my clit.

The tap causes me to jolt and him to groan.

His circles start of soft and slow, his finger slides down, and he pushes into my body, while he brings his thumb to my clit.

"Hold on Honey, you are going to come quick and hard." Cole whispers.

He starts to thrust in and out, making his thumb skim my swollen clit.

He adds a second finger and makes sure to hit my g-spot every time he thrusts in, which brings my orgasm on quick and hard, completely soaking his hand in my cum.

He withdraws is hand from my pants and brings them quickly up to his mouth.

He sucks both digits into his mouth and moans quietly.

I look into his eyes and whisper "I need to go to the bathroom."

"I'll be there in a bit. I want you ready to get naked and fucked hard on the counter when I get in there." Cole growls into my ear.

I nod my head, get up and move towards the bathroom.

I have been in the bathroom for about five minutes when he knocks and walks in.

He locks the door behind him and starts to undo his pants.

Erotic Bedtime Stories

"Honey, this has to be quick the movie is almost over, pants down and bend over." Cole demands.

I pull down my pants along with my panties, my anticipation level is high.

I hear a foil package and turn in time to see Cole rolling the condom down his long thick erection.

His eyes flash up to mine, and they are black with desire and lust.

I bend over thrust my ass out towards him and the sudden feel of his hand connecting with my ass, causing me to moan, and my body to tense.

In no time, his cock is being thrust into my tight, wet heat.

My orgasm is steaming through my body as he pounds out his own release.

I drop my head down to the counter and feel the coolness of the counter hit my cheek.

I hear his zipper being done up and then the door closing.

I turn my head to look at where he was standing, and he is gone. I just went through the equivalent of dine and dash.

I finish cleaning myself up and walk out into the crowd.

There he is standing with all his friends giving high fives to each other and standing in the middle is Shay with a huge grin on her face.

I turn my phone back on and send her a text.

Me: Glad I can be the fuck of your jokes. Don't contact me EVER!

I stand and watch as she checks her messages and watch her head snap up and scan the room until she finds me.

I give her the finger and mouth "Fuck You" and walk out the door.

In The Club of Submission

I've been sitting on this stool for all of three minutes, when he walks into the club.

He is absolutely gorgeous too, he looks to be about six-foot three with jet black styled short hair, he is built like a welterweight fighter. He is dressed in a pair of dress pants and a white top, or a light top, I can tell because his top is glowing under the black lights of the club.

I had come to the club with my friends to get away from the monotony of the daily grind.

They are out on the dance floor shaking what their Momma's gave them, and I just stopped to get a drink.

Since I am the designated driver I get the privilege of drinking pop or water.

Here's the thing, of my friends I am the curviest. I stand at five feet two inches and have curves in all the right places, my friends are all stick thin and gorgeous.

I'm brought out of my inner thoughts when the bartender places my glass down in front of me, he smiles and taps the bar before he walks away.

"That was weird." I mumble to myself as I take a sip of ice-cold water.

Just as I am finishing my pop I feel a hand land on the small of my back and looking to the side I see it's some greasy man, and by greasy, I mean his hair is literally dripping in it, his eyes are glazed over and focused on the cleavage that I am sporting and his breath smells like he was liking someone's asshole.

He smiles and just as he is about to say something another hand lands on my neck and his smell of citrus and clean invades my brain.

"Mine, piss off" is all the dark voice says.

His hand on my neck doesn't allow me to turn around, just to feel the muscular lines of his body as they press into my back.

The greasy man looks over my shoulder and his eyes widen in fear.

"Yeah-yeah-yeah man sorry I didn't know this beautiful woman was yours." He stutters.

"For tonight she is mine, what happens after that, we will see." The dark voice responds.

"Excuse me, who do you think you are? I'm not some cheap piece of meat." I yell.

"Next time you use that beautiful pouty mouth of yours the only words that will be coming out of it will be Yes Sir." Dark voice states.

"What the fuck are you talking about?" I yell again.

"Yes Sir, is the only thing that will be coming out of those pretty pouty lips." He growls into my ear.

I nod my head; his voice has made my panties melt, and my pussy slick.

"We are going to go out to my car, and head to my place, where you will do everything that I ask of you. Do you understand?" Dark voice asks.

I nod my head and then whisper, "Yes sir, I need to tell my friends that I am leaving."

He nods his head and then leans in and growls, "They already know, look."

My eyes swing to my friends on the dance floor, and they are in the same situation as me, each have a man with a hand on their necks, and they are all looking at me nodding at whatever their sirs are saying.

I stand up and finally get to see who my sir is, it's the man I noticed walking into the club.

His eyes are black; there is a tattoo on his neck that disappears into his collar and one on both hands that go into his sleeves. He links his fingers through mine as the group of us are guided out of the club.

I notice three high-end cars waiting out front, and each of my friends and I are guided to one.

He opens the door to a cheery red car and guides me to have a seat and then leans in and buckles my belt.

As he comes to my face he stares into my eyes and whispers "you will submit to my every need tonight, if that is too much, tell me now."

"I'm good Sir, what is your name?" I ask staring into his black lust filled eyes.

"You will address me as Sir, and I shall call you my beauty. That's it." He growls and I nod.

He closes the door to his car and walks towards the back. He is having a conversation with the guy in the car behind us, and all I can think about is his car smells like him or how wet my panties are.

I run my hands up and down my thighs slowly bringing my hands closer to the place that I need the most amount of pressure.

He opens his door and states into the cab "If your finger touches my pussy I will take my belt to those pretty little thighs and light them up red."

I stop and pull my hand away like I have been burned.

He guides himself into the car and starts it.

"Put your head back and close your eyes do not open them just listen to my voice as I describe how I am going to use your body tonight and tomorrow morning." He says.

I do as I'm told and lay back with my eyes close. I feel him grab my hand and place it on his crotch, and then he begins to tell me what he is going to do.

"First once we get to my house, you will not get out of the car until I have guided you out like, a proper gentleman, then once we get into my place you will strip all of your perfectly tight clothes off that delectable body, but you must leave

Erotic Bedtime Stories

on those sexy as fuck black heels. I plan
on having those digging into my back as I
feast on that intoxicating pussy I can
smell from here." I can feel his cock
growing with every word he says, just as
my stomach tightens and my cunt gushes.
I never thought you could have an orgasm
just from words, but he is about to make
it happen.

"Sir, when I need to may I please
come?" I whisper with my eyes still closed.

I hear him groan and lengthen. "Oh
god yes My Beauty, flood my car with
them smell of your sweet scent." He growls
and then continues his description.

"Second, I will have you kneel before
me with your knees spread wide open, so I
can see the honey pot that is hiding
between your legs, and I can see the
perfect handful of tits that are on your
chest. Does that make your nipples perk,
and your juices flow? Do you want my
eyes gazing over your body, taking in
everything that I will be feasting on?" He
questions me and all I can do is moan.

135

"I like that sound, third I will have you slowly undo my pants and take them off. Then you will take off my boxers, and slowly stroke my cock as it come into view. Once I'm naked you will drop your hands to your thighs, close your eyes and open those pretty pouty lips as I guide my swollen cock into your throat. You will not touch me, but you will allow me to fuck your face until I am ready to stop. Do you understand?" he says.

"Yes Sir" I whisper, and the tingles are building to an atomic proportion I am squirming in my seat and trying my best to get any relief that I can get.

"Once I have stopped, you will stand up and place yourself on the dining room table; this is where I will feast on your greedy pussy. I will have you squirting so many times that by the time I am done and ready to fuck this tight hole, you will be too exhausted to move and I will carry you to my bed where I will tie you to the frame spread eagle. You will be so tired but I will keep you awake by sliding my cock into your wet heat and fucking you for hours, bringing you multiple orgasms, making your voice..." I don't hear his next sentence as I scream out my pleasure from his words, flooding my panties with my come.

It takes me a few minutes to come back from seeing stars and catch my breath.

If this is how it's going to be with just his words, can you imagine how explosive the real thing will be?

Just as I get my breathing steady, my car door opens and Sir is standing there with a smirk on his face.

"Welcome to my home, when you get inside, I want your panties. Let's go have some fun, shall we?

I think to myself just before he closes the door that tomorrow and possibly well into next week I am going to be pleasantly sore in all the right places.

Let the pleasure begin!

Roadside Assistance

I have been standing beside my broke down car for the last three hours.

I called my local tow company as soon as the smoke started to overflow from under my hood.

Now I am at the point that I am in desperate need of getting off the side of the road.

I have called and talk to my Mother, my Brother and my Best friend. I have checked my social media accounts multiple times, plus have enjoyed reading two, yes two books by my favorite author and even got caught up on my sleep. Ok it was a fifteen minutes cat nap, but it was very refreshing.

I am slowly banging my head against the steering wheel when a tap comes at my window.

I jump and gasp in my seat as I slowly turn my head to look out my window.

Standing out in the late afternoon sun is this man; the only way to describe him is a Demi God like man glistening with sweat from the hot sun.

His hair is cut short and the color of chocolate, with eyes a piercing grayish blue. From under the sweat soaked t-shirt that is molded to his muscular frame I can see a six-pack and a very prominent pelvic muscle waiting to be licked and followed with my tongue and hand.

"Ms. Are you ok?" The man asks.

I am stuck in the fantasy of following his pelvic muscles with my tongue that I am startled when he knocks again and asks, "Ma'am are you ok?"

I slowly nod my head and take a deep breath, lowering the window only a crack I stutter out "Y-Y-Yes I'm ok, but my car is not."

"Ok Ms. My name is Kennedy, I'm sorry that it took so long to get here, can

you please pop the hood?" The man
named Kennedy asks.

I nod and release the hood.

I watch him closely as he stalks
towards the front of the car and lifts the
hood.

I start to take deep breaths to
steady my heart rate, so that I can step
out of my car to see what is actually wrong
with my car.

"So, Mr. Kennedy." I start to say.

"It's just Kennedy Ma'am." His
husky voice says which causes a flood in
my panties that I have no control over.

"Ok, Kennedy. What is going on with
my car?" I ask slowly losing my patience.

"Well, it's not good. It looks like you
did some damage to your engine. I am
going to need to have to tow it back to my
shop. Miss?" he tells me, as he asks for
my name.

"Oh, I'm so Sorry my name is Clara
Scarlet, but please call me Clara, because
if you call me Ma'am one more time my

flip-flop will go up your nose." I state and grab my purse out of the car.

I am coming around from the back of my car and I see Kennedy on the ground, he's looking under my car and looks like he is hooking up the chain to pull my car up onto the flatbed of the tow truck.

His whole body is up into a push up, and he is supporting his weight on his toes and his hands, but his eyes are focused on me, it is like her is staring into my soul and flicking my clit with his mind.

The intense stare down makes me rub my legs together like a praying mantis, but I am trying to get some relief.

I hear Kennedy growl and he is up and in front of me with his hands in my hair and pulling my head back to look up.

"Clara, you are driving me insane. My cock is so hard that my brain has no blood to function and all I can think about it swiping my tongue through your pussy as I taste you. I want to bend you over the trunk of your car and sink into your wet

141

willing heat. I want to savor every
whimper, moan and sigh that I make you
release, and then I want you to scream my
name as you soak my cock with your cum.
Do you want that?" Kennedy growls
against my lips.

My panties are soaked from the
arousal of his growled words.

I moan into his mouth as he pins
me to the side of the tow truck, slowly
grinding his bulge into my stomach.

"I can't wait Clara; I need you like I
need to breath. I want to strip you right
here and now, then slowly run my tongue
down your body. Can I?" Kennedy asks
and all I can do is nod.

His hands slowly start to move down
my arms and across my waist to the hem
of my shirt and slowly peels it up over my
head. His lips capture mine, and he drags
his tongue across my bottom lip, to my
jaw, and then slides it up to my ear where
he captures my lob and gently bites.

Before he continues he whispers
into my ear "this time and this time alone

Erotic Bedtime Stories

I will do you quick, I'll fuck you hard and make you cum no less than twice before I spray my cum across your ass. Then you will slide those sexy as fuck thongs on and sit in my cum until I can get you into the shower. Got it!" He bites my ear and then kisses and sucks his way down my neck to my shoulder.

His hands slowly slide up my sides, and he cups my breast and pinches my nipples through the lace of my bra. I moan and throw my head back.

He continues his assault on my body as he makes his way from my neck to the round globes of my boobs. As his tongue traces, long strokes across my breast his fingers nimbly undo my bra and slides it off my arms. His hands come back to my nipples, and he pinches them as he bites my tit, it causes me to spiral into an orgasm, and as my body shakes he slides my skirt up around my waist and moves my panties to the side and sucks my clit into his mouth as his tongue flicks on a steady beat.

143

I can feel another orgasm coming on, and I am starting to brace myself for the sudden rush, when he stops and stands up. The lack of contact from him causes me to moan and bring my eyes to his face.

The intensity of his stare captivates me and it's not until he demands, "Get on your knees and suck my cock Baby."

It's almost like he has me hypnotized by his thick erection, because one look and I have dropped to my knees and swallowed his cock down the back of my throat.

His groans push me to go faster and suck harder, bobbing my head up and down his shaft, slowly running my hands that have been clutching the cheeks of his ass and guiding them down as one cups and rolls his balls and the other slides between his ass cheeks as I start to stimulate the pucker of his asshole. I don't plan on sticking my finger in his ass, but as soon as I touch his whole he groans loudly and lengthens in my mouth, he is fucking my face as his hands are clamped on the sides of my head. As his hips rocked back and forth I place the tip of my finger so that is slides inside him just a little and then remove my finger and trail it gently back through his legs.

"Clara, I need your pussy wrapped around my cock, now!" he yells.

I suck hard and push his hips back so that he pops from my mouth.

I slowly stand and watch as he bends and grabs a foil packet out of his wallet.

His teeth tear the package and takes the rubber out then slides it over his erection, making sure that he has a little space at the tip.

His eyes come up to meet my lust filled eyes, and he twirls his hands and demands "spin around and present me with that gorgeous round ass."

With no hesitation, I spend and bend slightly at the waist pushing my ass towards Kenned.

With no time to adjust to Kennedy's size he slams his cock deep inside me and starts to pound out his rhythm. The orgasm that he had me nearing with his tongue, flies through my body and has me clenching tightly around his cock.

"That's right Babe cum on my cock, make me lose control, oh fuck yeah keep cumming! Yes!" Kennedy growls.

The mixture of Kennedy encouraging me to come and his constant motion, add in the fact that he has slides his hand around and attacks my click, which causes me to see stars and cum so hard that I squirt all over him as he slides back in to finish himself off.

His strokes start to slow I can feel his legs start to shake as he collapses on my back.

We stand there on the side of the road slowly catching our breaths, when we hear the 'whoop' of a police siren.

"Babe, you have about fifteen seconds to get dressed, or we will be jailed for indecent exposure.

Erotic Bedtime Stories

I quickly pull apart and get dressed. The condom is knotted, and he places it in my purse which is lying open on the ground.

I scrunch up my nose and look at him, his eyes have a crinkle in them and his shoulders are bouncing.

"Once we get back to my garage, I'll take it out and place it where all our other ones will be. I am nowhere near finished with your tasty pussy." He states and slaps my ass on his way to talk to the officer.

I watch his ass as he walks away and think to myself, I am glad that he is my tow truck driver.

147

Under My Thumb

I am walking up to my best friend's dorm; my best friend is a guy. He is absolutely amazing and so supportive of me.

I get to his dorm door and don't bother to knock; I stride in and stop dead in my tracks.

He is lying on his bed on his stomach in nothing but underwear. His body is firm and his ass is tight. I never thought that my pussy would get wet from my best friend, but standing here and watching him listening to music as he shakes his ass is like an erotic fantasy come to life.

I can imagine him dominating me and forcing me to submit to his every whim.

How he would take control and show me that the rumors about him are one hundred percent true.

"Natalie, are you ok?" I hear his voice.

I snap my darkened eyes to him and see his eyes roaming over my body. I am dressed to go to the party that we are going to. He was supposed to be ready, but he is still so gloriously not.

I see him approach me, and he runs his nose up my neck and whispers in my ear "finally seeing what has been under your thumb are you?"

I gasp and step back hitting the wall behind me.

He has a smirk on his face and I watch as his hand comes towards my face.

"I see you Nat; you have been on my mind since we were seventeen. It's your face I see when I cum with the others. Do you finally see me?" Jenson asks.

"You. Want. Me?" I stutter.

"I want to own you, I want you to submit to me and let me be your Dom. I want your orgasms, your sighs and moans to be only for me. Are you willing to do that?" He growls, I nod my head.

"Words Natalie, I need to hear your sinful voice." He whispers.

"Y-y-yes Jenson, please" I squeak.

"This means, we are an item, you are my sub, my woman. No more other men unless I see fit, but no one will touch my pussy, that's right Natalie you are mine therefore your beautiful bouncing tits and your tight sopping wet cunt are mine. If I want to finger you at the back of the lecture hall I will. Got it?" he states.

"Yes" I say.

"Now, you will refer to me as King when we are in a scene." He informs me.

"Yes" I say my voice getting a little firmer, he quirks his eyebrow at me.

"Yes, King" I try again.

"Good my Princess, now take off your clothes, your kings cock needs to be serviced." He demands.

I stare at him unsure, he doesn't say anything just steps back and places his hands on his hips.

I don't think any more, I just get rid of my dress. He groans because taking off the dress leaves me naked. I couldn't wear a bra or panties because the dress was too tight and hugged me in all the right places.

"You were going to go with me to the frat party and have nothing on?" he growls.

I nod and whisper "Yes, King."

"On your knees Princess, spread your legs and let me stare at your delicious pussy. I can smell the sweet scent of your arousal, and it's making my cock leak." He states in and demanding ton as a wet spot formed on the front of his underwear.

I drop to my knees and spread my legs wide, and because I am a little bit embarrassed at how turned on I am, I drop my eyes to the floor and place my hands palms down on my legs.

151

"Natalie look up at me sweet pea."
Jenson whispers.

I bring my head up and look into the
eyes of my best friend, who as of ten
minutes ago has become my man.

"Are you ok?" He asks me as he
crouches down.

"Yes King, I am fine" I say and watch
lust darken his eyes.

"In the future, I want you to think of
three words that you can remember. One
word will be for me to stop, one will mean
that you are nervous but continue with
caution and one gives me the green light
to continue what I am doing. Ok?" He says
as his finger runs down my cheek.

"Ok" I say and then watch as he
stands up and rids himself of his
underpants, his cock bounces in my face
but out of reach of my mouth.

"I get to cum first; this is for wasting
four years of me being able to have your
pussy. Open your mouth and swallow my
cock. Do not waste any of my seed as it

shoots from my tip." He demands and thrusts his cock towards my mouth.

I open and allow him to slide in deep. I have no gag reflex, so when I look into his eyes as he watches me swallow his cock, it makes me wetter.

It takes ten minutes and a lot of saliva, and then he is shouting my name as his cum fills my mouth and slides down my throat.

"Your turn, stand up and go to the bed. Bring your legs to your chest and use your arms to hold them apart." He demands through pants of breath.

I follow his direction and lie on the bed, bringing my legs up to my chest and hold them there. The air in the room chills my hot core as my excitement floods my pussy more.

I hear him walk to the desk beside his bed and open the drawer, taking out a small butt plug and a bottle of lube.

"This is all new, I just bought this one." He says and smiles.

I smile back at him and watch as he prowls to the end of the bed.

I feel the bed dip and then stars start to explode.

His mouth is on my pussy sucking and nipping at the lips like a starved man. His tongue pokes out and laps at my juices, he takes his teeth and gently bites down on my clit causing my arms to let go of my legs.

"Now Princess, keep a hold of those perfect legs for me. I will stop what I am doing." He tells me from between my spread legs. My arousal is coating his lips like lip gloss.

I hooked my arms around my legs again, and he latches onto my clit and sucks hard. I cum flooding his mouth with orgasm, and he swallows it all.

I hear a cap open and feel coldness run down my ass. It causes me to shiver.

I feel the anal plug at the pucker of my asshole and before I can say anything his mouth is back in my pussy. His tongue is hard and demanding. My clit still sensitive from the first orgasm pulses under his tongue causing me to wiggle my hips.

He bites me again and I break apart with another intense orgasm.

During the orgasm, he slides the anal plug into my ass and is up on his knees, seethed in a condom and pushing into my clenching channel.

He doesn't move, his hard cock is sitting inside me and my orgasm is starting to die down. I open my eyes to see what he is doing and watch as he stares into my eyes with a smile on his face.

"My girl tastes like nectar. Princess are you ready?" He whispers and pulls almost all the way out and slides back in.

"This is going to be hard, we need to get to the party and I want everyone to see the freshly fucked face you'll have, so they all know that we are together and that no one comes to take you from me." He growls and then starts to pound in and out of my pussy.

The movement of his legs keep a steady pace of hitting the plug and sends me barreling into an intense orgasm that has me holding my breath and pushing, squirting all over his stomach and pushing the butt plug out.

I watch with fascination as Jenson rips off the condom and strokes his release over my thighs and pussy.

He collapses on top of me and my legs fall down. I have no feeling in my arms and my breathing is as erratic as his.

He wiggles his body rubbing his cum and my release into our thighs and then places a kiss on my lips.

"I want my girl marked with my cum tonight. I want every guy at this party to know that you have been claimed." He whispers and smiles.

"Get dressed my Nat, I can't wait to dance with you and be able to slide my cock into you from behind as people watch us fuck and dance. Then I plan on sitting on the couch with you on sitting on my

Erotic Bedtime Stories

cock, while I spread your legs and show
every guy at the party that your sweet
pink pussy is mine and mine alone." He
growls and then gets off me and slides his
underwear back in place.

By the time that the feeling has
come back to my arms and legs, Jenson is
already dressed and helping me off the
bed.

The bulge in his pants indicates that
he is ready to go again. I look at him and
ask "Did you take Viagra? You know if you
have an erection for longer than four
hours you need to see a doctor."

I chuckle and slide my dress over
my body.

"I don't need medication to get an
erection. Just knowing that you are mine,
and we are a couple makes Pedro and
happy one eyes snake." He chuckles.

"Pedro, really?" I ask him now falling
into a full sit of the giggles.

He smiles and wraps his arms
around my waist.

"Yeah Babe, we are going to be forever, even your giggle makes my balls fill with sperm." He whispers and then kisses me.

We leave the dorm and head for the party.

Tonight, has been the best night and I can't wait for more.

The Dance

I HAVE BEEN ON THIS dance floor, with my girls for at least an hour.

My girls consist of a five-foot nine inches, blonde haired, crystal blue-eyed bombshell the size of a Victoria's Secret model, so tiny waist and double D boobs. The there's an athletic five feet five inches, jet black haired and emerald green eyes with size E tits.

I'm the short curvy chick with spiked brown hair and grayish blue eyes. I have a wicked sense of humor and an outlook on life that keeps me living in the moment. My body maybe curvaceous, my boobs make my body look weird.

My two friends have had a bunch of guys hanging off of them since we got on the dance floor. The faces they make when a new one grabs their hips and pulls them closer to his body is hilarious. They have even with the cock measurements by how big their mouths open.

I am laughing my ass off at the new set of guys that have attached themselves to my friends when their eyes go big, their mouths hang open, and they completely stop dancing.

When I go to step forward I feel a hand move down my back lightly and then across my hips until they find purchase on my full waist.

"Turn around and face me, my beautiful Spiked Queen." A low husky growl sounded in my ear.

I slowly spin around and my face meets a broad chest. As I slowly raise my head to the face of a beautiful Adonis. I start to take in little details, like a red, yellow and orange flame like wing tattoo with the tip of the wing ending just under his ear, and two, two inch gauges settled nicely in his ear lobes.

On the corner of his mouth is a small lip ring and as my eyes connect with his mouth he licks his lips and I see a shiny metal barbell in his tongue, which causes me to shiver. Then my eyes connect with his silver eyes and I gasp.

"Hi, my Queen, you going to dance with me and let me do anything I want to you right here on the dance floor. If you start to protest I will stop and walk away, but I will warn every single cocksucker in the place that you are my Queen and Flame does not share his toys at all. Do you understand me?" He whispers to me. I do the only thing I can and nod.

He smirks at me and spins me back around, then he lowers his tall frame and cradles my ass in his pelvis and starts to slowly grind on me.

My arousal is slicking my pussy and because my skirt is short and tight I have gone commando so my juices are coating my inner thighs.

His hands start a slow sensual roam undoing a few buttons on my tight top, and slowly sliding up to my breasts which he cups and slowly rolls my pebbled nipples between his finger and thumb taking the rough lace of my bra and rubbing it along the flesh of my nipples.

He slowly moves one hand and grasps my hip and drags my body flush with his hips, grinding his steel erection into my ass.

"My cock has been rock hard since the first twirl of your hips. It's embarrassing talking to my brother's constantly adjusting the lead pipe in my pants. I will come in you hard within the next hour, you are to accept it and keep your eyes on your girls. Two of my brother's will be doing the exact same as me, I want your girls to your orgasm face and I want every other prick in this place to know you are branded by me inside and out." He whispers in my ear. I nod and gasp as he pinches my nipples hard.

A slow song comes on, and he spins me around bringing my pebbled nipples that are now poking through the holes he ripped in the lace.

Erotic Bedtime Stories

"Your first orgasm will only be for
me, keep your eyes locked on mine while
my finger slowly enters your body." He
whispers against my lips and then slowly
slides his tongue along my bottom lip
causing me to gasp and him to deepen the
kiss.

I feel his hand guide its way down
the front of me and slide up under my
short skirt.

It doesn't take long for him to have
ripped my panties off and tucked them
into his back pocket, and then bring his
hand back to the apex of my thighs.

"Your pussy is slick with need, but
remember your first orgasm is mine." He
growls and applies a rough pressure with
two fingers on my clit. Tingles race down
my spine and cause me to gasp in air and
flare my eyes which are still locked on his.

He guides his fingers lower through
my slit, and pushes them inside me. He
brings his mouth to my ear and whispers
"you will come in thirty seconds or I will
turn you around and watch while I slap

this beautiful peach shaped ass until its
fire engine red. Get me?" I nod.

He grins and bends his finger and
starts to push in and out of my hot cunt
hitting my g spot and sending waves of hot
tingles through my body.

Thirty seconds is literally all it took
for my orgasm to rip through my body
causing my mouth to fall open readying
for a moan, but his mouth is on mine
swallowing down the guttural groan that
just flew out of my throat.

"That was hot, now it's time for
orgasm number two and you will face your
girls and all watch each other's orgasms
and enjoy what me and my brothers do,"
he states and spins me around.

My girl's faces are all flushed and
their eyes are twinkling with lust. I watch
as both men bend down and latch onto
their necks. The guys hands are still
under their skirts slowly start to slide out
only to shoot to the back and I watch as
the lift the back of their skirts exposing
my friend's asses to their hips. Then just

as I watch the guys lean in and whisper in my friend's ears, my own bad ass hot guy whispers. "Reach behind you and undo the zipper on my jeans, then reach in a pull my cock out. I'm going to fuck you for your next orgasm, then we will go to the booth and finish because what I want to do is going to be difficult while we are standing."

I follow his orders and focus back on my friends as both their eyes roll and then my eyes roll. Flame has adjusted us so that his cock is deep inside me and within five deep strokes I cum on his cock and my body starts to crumble, only to be caught by Flame.

"Your cunt gets really tight when you cum, now it's time for you to use your mouth on me while I discuss some business with my brothers." He states and leads me towards a booth in the back. I look over my shoulder and see that both my friends are coming with the guys that they are with.

Flame slides in the booth and demands "get on your knees under the table and suck my cock until I tell you different."

I don't know what it is but his command sets my pussy to drip, and I find myself instantly dropping and crawling under the table.

He already has his pants undone and his erection is pointing at me and my mouth started to water.

I am so in the zone and focused on Flames cock that I don't notice my friends crawling under the table and positioning themselves in front of the guys that they were dancing with.

Flames hand comes under the table and grabs the back of my head and moves me towards his purple head, without hesitation I open my mouth over his hard-on and slide him all the way to the back of my throat.

His leg stiffens and his hips thrust up and hit the back of my throat. I retract my head and on the up glide I hollow out my checks and suck hard.

I don't need him to tell me he is coming because his cock thickens, his legs stiffen and his hand in my hair clinches as hot cum shoots from his cock.

I feel his legs shake and wonder if that's it for tonight.

I sit back on my feet and let my head hang, what in the hell am I doing?

Flame's hand in my hair pulls me up towards the seat, and as he releases my hair he taps the seat beside him.

"You're done tonight, get your shit and leave." He demands.

I stare at him slack jawed.

"I beg your pardon?" I growl at him and narrow my eyes.

"Bitch move, I got what I wanted." He shouts.

I can't believe this shit, what a fucking douche.

I stand up and fix my skirt and head towards the door, we are just getting ready to leave when he comes up to me and stats "I'll see you next time."

I spin around and narrow my eyes before I yell "Like fucking hell you won't come near me again. I hope your dick falls of from scabies and you have to learn to suck a dick, you, useless piece of shit!"

With that I walk out and jump into the cab, telling the driver to take me home.

About The Author

JA resides in Northern Ontario Canada but is originally from the Capital of Ontario.

She is a married to her loving husband and has three beautiful children.

When she is not locked in her writing cave she works with the board of education as a supply Educational Assistant.

She loves watching hockey and Soccer and enjoys talking to the many people she has made friends with.

She enjoys a good joke and can usually be seen with a smile on her face and a joke on her lips.

Contact The Author

Facebook
https://www.facebook.com/authorjalafrance/
Goodreads
https://www.goodreads.com/author/show/149
51067.J_A_Lafrance

Instagram
https://www.instagram.com/ja_lafrance
Twitter
https://www.twitter.com/ja_lafrance

BookBub
https://www.bookbub.com/profile/ja-
lafrance?list=author_books
Readers Group
https://www.facebook.com/groups/135174478
8198642/

Email
jalafranceauthor@gmail.com
Website
http://jalafrance.wixsite.com/website

Made in the USA
Middletown, DE
04 March 2021